Horse Camp

~ A ~ Horse Girl Mystery

by Carrie Seim
Illustrations by Steph Waldo

Penguin Workshop

For every horse person, young or old.
May you ride bravely through life exactly as you are.
May you gallop after your dreams, no matter how wild.
May your heart remain untamed.
—CS

PENGUIN WORKSHOP
An imprint of Penguin Random House LLC
1745 Broadway, New York, New York 10019

First published in the United States of America by Penguin Workshop,
an imprint of Penguin Random House LLC, 2025

Text copyright © 2025 by Carrie Seim
Illustrations copyright © 2025 by Penguin Random House LLC

Map and heart-bar illustrations by Ron Baird
Emoji (used throughout): calvindexter/DigitalVision Vectors/Getty Images

Penguin Random House values and supports copyright. Copyright fuels creativity, encourages diverse voices, promotes free speech, and creates a vibrant culture. Thank you for buying an authorized edition of this book and for complying with copyright laws by not reproducing, scanning, or distributing any part of it in any form without permission. You are supporting writers and allowing Penguin Random House to continue to publish books for every reader. Please note that no part of this book may be used or reproduced in any manner for the purpose of training artificial intelligence technologies or systems.

PENGUIN is a registered trademark and PENGUIN WORKSHOP is a trademark of
Penguin Books Ltd, and the W colophon is a registered trademark of Penguin Random House LLC.

Visit us online at penguinrandomhouse.com.

Library of Congress Cataloging-in-Publication Data is available.

Printed in the United States of America

ISBN 9780593754009

1st Printing

LSCC

Design by Mary Claire Cruz
Series design by Julia Rosenfeld

This book is a work of fiction. Any references to historical events, real people, or real places are used fictitiously. Other names, characters, places, and events are products of the author's imagination, and any resemblance to actual events or places or persons, living or dead, is entirely coincidental.

The publisher does not have any control over and does not assume any
responsibility for author or third-party websites or their content.

The authorized representative in the EU for product safety and compliance is Penguin Random House Ireland, Morrison Chambers, 32 Nassau Street, Dublin D02 YH68, Ireland, https://eu-contact.penguin.ie.

CHAPTER ONE

My hands cling tightly to Bandit's reins as we bound down the forest path, his swift hooves carrying us farther away from Juniper Ranch.

Galumph, galumph, ga—booooooooom.

Bandit's ears swivel back, and he screeches to a halt. A deep rumble growls in the distance.

"Too much alfalfa again?" I whisper.

Bandit tosses his flaxen mane, clearly unimpressed by my joke.

"There's no reason to be nervous, boy," I say, the words tumbling out of my mouth.

I scan the ground around us with the flashlight my dad forced me to pack. ("Why do I need to bring a ginormous flashlight to summer camp when I already have a phone??" I'd whined. "You'll thank me later, Willa," he'd sighed. Ugh, please don't tell him his dad-tuition was right!) Sweeping the beam of light across the trail, I search frantically for the hoofprints I *know* must be nearby.

Bandit, my beloved steed for the summer, responds with an indignant *pfffffffft*.

"Yes, I know we're not supposed to leave camp. Especially after dark. Especially alone. Especially without telling anyone. *Especially*—"

BAAA-BOOOOM!!

We both nearly leap out of our skin as a deafening clap of thunder rattles across the canyon. I feel the muscles in Bandit's neck tense; he paws at the ground as his ears prick sharply forward, like a bull's—all sure signs he's about to spook. I lean forward to stroke his crest, trying to soothe him.

"Especially when a storm might be coming," I breathe, attempting to sound calm. (Even though I absolutely, positively do *not* feel calm!) I tuck my flashlight away, then steal a glance at the herd of clouds that are now stampeding across the full moon.

"Look, those thunderheads are still on the other side of the mountain," I say, forcing my voice into a cheerful, *everything-is-totally-under-control* register. "We've got plenty of time to find that horse and make it back safe and sound before—"

CRACK!!!

A burst of lightning explodes like fireworks above the canopy of pine trees that tower over us.

"Before anyone notices we're gone," I finish, swallowing

hard. "Okay, so maybe the storm is getting a *teeny-tiny* bit closer? Have I mentioned I am *not* a meteorologist??"

I look down to see Bandit's reins trembling in my clammy hands. It appears that *I* am now the one who needs soothing. I take a deep breath of the suffocatingly heavy air, hoping to slow my galloping heart. Then I let out a *click-click* to get him moving again.

But Bandit is no fool. He has zero interest in waiting around for the skies to open up. Centuries of instinct have taught him to be terrified of lightning. (He is also terrified of—in no particular order—butterflies, puddles, buckets, large hats, and any leaf that has the audacity to land in his path. But at the moment? We're focused on the lightning.)

Bandit pulls hard at his reins, skittering sideways and attempting to make a U-turn back toward home.

"Come on, boy," I grunt, nudging his ribs and battling him in a tug-of-war. "I know you want your bag of oats just as much as I want my midnight s'mores. But if we don't move quickly, the storm will wash away those hoofprints—and our only chance of finding our friend!"

Bandit flings his head back longingly to the safety of camp and his cozy stall. But before he can bolt, we both hear the sickening, high-pitched squeal of a horse in the distance.

Heeeeeeeeeeeee!!!

"He's in *serious* danger!" I plead, my voice turning raspy as I fight the panic growing inside me. Then I look down and whisper, "And we may be his last chance."

Chapter Two

A few weeks ago . . .

Pfffffffft.

Clyde Lee snorts dreamily as I rub a curry comb in short circles over his flanks. He could use some sprucing up after he spent the afternoon playing "Let's Make Dirt Angels!" in the paddock with the other horses of Oakwood Riding Academy.[1]

Clyde is half Clydesdale, half thoroughbred, and 100 percent ginormous—his hooves are each the size of a medium pizza! He has whipped-cream-white feathers on three of his fetlocks and a vanilla-colored blaze down his muzzle—which now looks decidedly *chocolate*-colored. Although he's now officially retired from teaching young riders like me, as the honorary mascot of Oakwood, he still manages to keep busy.

---

[1] A paddock is a fenced area where horses can hang out, exercise, and get a snack . . . or roll in the dirt, as the case may be!

His hectic schedule includes flinging himself in the muck, rolling vigorously, and shaking off onto anyone who might be strolling nearby.² Which today, happens to be me.

"Guess I forgot to take my dirt shower this morning," I laugh, plucking dried bits of hay and pebbles from my dark frizzy hair, which I've braided into two tight halos on top of my head. "Do you really have to go for a roll *every* day, boy?"

Clyde nickers cheekily, then nudges me with his muddy muzzle. He's ready for his spa appointment to continue!

I shake my head in exasperation, then reach for the grooming bucket in the corner of his stall, fishing out a dandy brush. Although this was *not* part of my plan for the day, I can't resist Clyde Lee's giant, hopeful eyes. He's my favorite four-legged creature on the planet, my ridiculous partner in crime, my forever heart-horse.

Before we moved to Nebraska and I started taking riding lessons last year, I'd spent my entire life (fourteen whole years!) collecting Breyer model horses, wearing breeches to school, drawing stallions in my notebook, and *dreaming* of someday becoming a real #HorseGirl.

Then? When my parents let me sign up for classes at Oakwood and I met Clyde Lee? It actually happened.

---

2 Horses roll in the dirt for many reasons—to scratch an itch, give themselves a massage, cool down their coats, or celebrate how gosh-darn happy they are. Fun fact: Rolling in horses is a lot like yawning in people—it's contagious! If you see one horse stop, drop, and roll, just wait for the others to join him. (Thanks a lot, Clyde Lee.)

Clyde showed me how to walk and trot and canter and soar—*majestically!*—over jumps. Okay, so he also frequently screeched to a halt, sending me flying—*braces first!*—into the dirt. But my instructor, Georgia, says you're not a true horse girl until you take a few tumbles. So . . . mission accomplished!

Eventually, I even got invited to join the Oakwood Flyers, the stable's elite jumping team. And now that the super-stressful school year's over? I get to spend my entire summer at the stable with my forever herd of friends—girl, boy, and equine!

For the first time in my life, I feel like I can finally, *finally* exhale.

Phewwwwww.

Which is exactly the moment Georgia's voice rattles through the barn speakers. "Attention, Oakwood Flyers—rustle up in the indoor arena for an important meeting," she announces. "Lickety-split."

Uh-oh. Did I *phewwwwww* way too soon??

But I know better than to keep Georgia waiting. So I fling the dandy brush back into the grooming bucket, give Clyde a quick kiss on his mud-caked muzzle, make sure his stall door is firmly latched, then hustle toward the ring.

"I'll be back as soon as I can, boy!" I call over my shoulder as Clyde lets out an indignant *pfffffffft* to let me know how unfair it is that he isn't invited to the party.

When I reach the arena, I spot my three best friends, the

Claremont triplets, leaning against the bars of the metal fence that divides the parent bleacher area from the dirt riding ring. The blond sisters may *seem* identical to the untrained eye, but after a year of taking riding lessons with them? I know they're anything but.

First there's Gwyneth, who was born two minutes before Everleigh and seven minutes before Noel. Gwyneth takes her responsibilities as the "big sister" extremely seriously. On show days, she makes sure everyone packs sunscreen and fly spray and extra snacks . . . for the horses *and* ourselves. Gwyn decided earlier this year that she wants to become an equine veterinarian—aka a doctor for horses, aka the coolest type of doctor in the history of doctors!

Standing next to her—except upside down—is Everleigh. In case it wasn't obvious, along with horses, Ev is super into gymnastics. She kills time while we "hurry up and wait" at jumping competitions by practicing handstands and cartwheels and back walkovers and front tucks. She says they help her stay focused and energized. I guess it's true, because she jumps fences almost as high as she triple flips![3]

Last in the lineup—but right side up—is Noel. (It's easy to tell it's Noel, because she wears glasses. Not because she

---

[3] Show jumping obstacles come in different styles and heights, depending on the level of competition. The biggest Olympic jumps are more than five feet tall. But in 1949, a thoroughbred stallion named Huaso set a world record, jumping over a fence more than *eight* feet high. (That's even taller than me and Clyde!)

needs them, but because she got tired of everybody mixing her up with her sisters.) Noey is obsessed with mystery books. She's convinced—and a little nervous—that danger could be lurking around every corner!

Just as I'm about to ask if they know anything about this mysterious Important Meeting, my former frenemy, Amara (aka Queen of the #HorseGirls), sashays into the arena. Her magnificent glossy ponytail swishes behind her in perfect time with her elegant strides.

"Move it or lose it, breeches," she singsongs.

Like the Claremont triplets, Amara has been riding since she was practically a baby, and has enough money to afford her own horse. But *unlike* the Claremont triplets, she's always reminding me of those facts. Still, Amara convinced her mom to pay for Clyde to stay at Oakwood after he retired, so I'll always be grateful to her for that. Way down deep, Amara actually has a giant heart. (Just don't tell anyone!)

As for the other Oakwood Flyers, Luis Valdez and Gray Dawson? They decided to go to surf camp in California right after school ended. (Why anyone would choose to spend their summer falling off a boogie board when they could be falling off a bucking horse is beyond me.)

Anyway, once we're all gathered in the arena, Georgia strides toward us from the other side of the ring. Her heavy boots thud forebodingly in the dirt, echoing off the barn's worn wooden rafters. She pauses for a moment in front of the metal fence we're leaning on, and we each instinctively straighten up. Including Everleigh, who springs from her hands to her feet.

"This isn't easy to say," Georgia drawls, kicking the toe of her boot through the dirt. "So I'm just gonna go ahead and spit it out."

I glance nervously at the other Flyers as Georgia waves her hand toward the beams of sunlight streaming through several holes in the arena roof. "This old barn's crumblin' faster than my peach cobbler."

I normally get excited anytime someone mentions dessert . . . but something in her voice tells me to put away the whipped cream.

"We've got more termites than students," she mutters, almost as if she's trying to convince herself of something. "I have no choice."

Georgia lets out a heavy sigh.

"I'm gonna have to close down Oakwood."

CHAPTER THREE

OMG. OMG. OMG.

I squeeze my eyes shut and will myself to wake up from this terrible dream. I thought I just heard Georgia say that she's GONNA HAVE TO CLOSE DOWN OAKWOOD.

And that can't possibly be true. Because if she's GONNA HAVE TO CLOSE DOWN OAKWOOD? It means my brief life as an official horse girl is officially *over*.

"Now, wait just a darn second," Georgia says, when she notices the shocked expressions exploding on all of our faces. "It's only for the summer! We're boarding all the horses at another stable for a few months while I get this placed fixed up. But we'll be back in business by fall. There's absolutely no need for y'all to worry."

Spoiler alert? This y'all was *extremely* worried.

"Just for the summer" may not seem long to most people.

But for a horse girl? Who'd planned to spend her entire summer at the stable??

It's a freaking eternity!

A few days after Georgia's ominous announcement, I drag myself to Oakwood for our final lesson before the barn doors officially close.

Even when I'm flying around the sunny outdoor arena on Minnie—the small-but-speedy dappled Welsh Cob I've been riding now that Clyde Lee is retired—I feel gutted. My shoulders slump with a heavy sadness, and I find it nearly impossible to "sit snooty" in my saddle.[1]

But as I glance around the riding ring, I notice something strange. All the other Flyers seem to be smiling and giggling and "sitting snooty" like everything is completely normal.

As the homemade horse T-shirt I'm wearing says, *WHAT THE HAY???*

That's when I overhear the Claremont triplets and Amara buzzing about something called Juniper.

Juniper, Juniper, Juniper—the word zips around the ring like a lightning bug, prompting squeals of joy whenever it materializes, oh-so-fleetingly. I have no idea what all the

---

[1] "Sit snooty" is Georgia's way of reminding me to keep my head up and chest out until I actually reach a jump. All I have to do is pretend I'm Amara with her pin-straight snobby posture—works like a charm!

squealing is about, because—as I may have mentioned before—I am a "novice" rider, aka "inexperienced," aka "Peasant of the #HorseGirls."

Eventually, though, I work up the courage to ask.

"So, um, what's this Juniper thing?" I mumble, as I dismount from Minnie.

"Willa, you literally can't be serious??" Amara whips her head around in disbelief. Her glossy ponytail quickly follows, smacking her cheek. Then her horse, a gorgeous black jumper named Silver Streak, twirls around for good measure, stomping the ground incredulously.

"Um . . . no? I mean yes! I mean—"

Amara cuts off my stammering to ask-slash-answer her own question. "Juniper Ranch is only *the* most epic horse camp in the entire country?"

She takes a long pause. "If not *the world*?!"

Amara's eyebrows remain poised high, as if this fact were common #HorseGirl knowledge and if I didn't know it, I should probably just turn in my breeches. Fortunately, the Claremont triplets swoop in to save me.

"It's this amazing sleepaway camp in Colorado!" Gwyneth explains.

"They have tons of horses *and* riders?" Everleigh gushes, the words flipping out of her mouth like a tumbling pass. "And since Georgia is closing Oakwood for the summer, our parents said we could go!"

"Wills, you *have* to come," Noel adds breathlessly. "If you sign up soon, maybe you can still get a spot in our cabin!" (Then she peeks over her glasses and whispers, "We're hoping it's not too deep in the forest . . . where the bears lurk.")

Her sisters nod enthusiastically. Even Amara gives me a half shrug of approval. Gwyneth dashes back to the stable and her tack trunk, then presses a Juniper Ranch Horse Camp flyer into my hands.

The brochure's grinning, flush-faced riders and sun-dappled horses all look so wildly happy—even the kids shoveling manure into a wheelbarrow look like they're exploding with joy.

That's when it hits me: *Of course* all the other Oakwood Flyers have a backup plan. And *of course* I'm the last one to know.

I suddenly realize that my entire forever herd—girl, boy, and equine—is about to disappear for the entire summer.

Without me.

After our lesson, I run home as fast as my gangly legs will carry me, waving the Juniper Ranch flyer in the air and begging my dad to sign me up. *Immediately*.

Unfortunately, my dad *immediately* flips to the back page of the brochure, drumming his finger on the camp's price tag.

"Whooeee, this place looks pretty fancy, Wills," he says with a whistle.

Ugh. After fourteen years in this family, I know that "pretty fancy" is dad-speak for "no way in heck can we afford that."

"If your horse pals won't be around, maybe you can dog-sit, kiddo!" he cheerfully suggests. He spends the next half hour trying to convince me that pooper-scoopering after our next-door neighbor's Great Dane will be just as fun as horse camp. "We've got plenty of manure to shovel right here at home!"

Blergh.

So I turn to FaceTime, beaming my large, pleading eyes to my mom, who's nine time zones away.

"Please, Mom? All my friends are going to camp! Pretty, pretty, *prettiest* please???" I whine, before adding the kicker: "I miss you."

My mom's a pilot in the air force, and she's currently deployed on the other side of the world, while my dad and my big sister, Kay, and I "hold down the fort" (as my dad insists on calling it) back in Nebraska. My mom's been gone for almost an *entire* year. Including Christmas. And my birthday. And Flag Day.

I know it's a really big deal that my mom's a pilot—it's a huge accomplishment and an honor, *et ceterahhh*. But I also really, really, *really* miss her every single day. Especially on days like today. (And also Flag Day!)

Unfortunately, despite my pretty-pleases, my mom just shakes her head and gives me the old "Sorry, sweetheart, maybe next year" speech. She says Juniper Ranch isn't in the budget this summer, especially since we have to pay for Kay's engineering camp.

Only my supersmart big sister would choose to spend her summer programming robots to eat algae. And only my parents would decide that RobotFest was somehow more important than horse camp.

I know we don't have as much money as the other families at Oakwood. And I know Kay's science stuff is super important. (Supposedly.) So I pretend I'm not upset about missing out on the best summer of my life.

But inside? *I'm pretty freaking upset!!*

After moving from place to place and feeling like the new kid weirdo my entire life, I finally found my passion *and* my forever herd. Why would my parents want me to lose all that? My friends will probably completely forget I exist by the time they get back from camp. It'll be like starting all over. And all the hard work I put into becoming a real horse girl will be for nothing.

Which is why I am back in the stable the next morning, holding back waves of tears as I groom Clyde Lee, trying to steal a few more moments with him before he (and everyone else I know) abandons me for the summer.

I use the dandy brush to sweep away all the dirt and grime the curry comb lifted from his coat. I also try to sweep away the burning disappointment that's been stirred up in my insides. But it doesn't seem to be working.

"You won't forget about me, right, boy?" I ask, my voice cracking.

Clyde, however, appears to have been hypnotized into a stone sculpture as I massage the brush through his gleaming coat.

"Right, boy??" I repeat, a little louder this time.

Eventually, he lets out a relaxed *pffffffffft.*

I'll take that as a yes. (Even if he's probably just gassy from all the apples I've been sneaking him to make sure he doesn't forget about me.)

After I finish combing out his mane and tail, I throw my arms around his giraffe-like neck. Or at least I attempt to—even for a "Wow You're Tall for a Girl" girl, I'm still not quite tall enough to reach the top of towering Clyde Lee, who is several hands taller than any other horse at Oakwood.[2] But he humors me by lowering his head, and I quickly swoop in for a hug.

---

[2] While humans are measured in feet, horses are measured in hands—a fun fact that can be traced back to ancient Egypt. Clydesdales can tower up to twenty hands tall, which comes out to about six and a half feet. And that's measuring only to the horse's withers (aka shoulders)! I'm not exactly that tall, but I still have some growing to do. *(Ugh!)*

"I'm going to miss you so much," I whisper into his mane.

Then—just as I start blubbering hot tears and snot into his freshly groomed coif—I notice a square of paper fluttering in the back of his stall. I scurry over to investigate, worried it might startle my gentle giant.

And that's when I see an envelope . . . scrawled with a big purple *W*. My hands begin to tremble as I carefully slide out a scrap of paper and unfold it:

> Dear Willa,
> You've worked hard all year,
> And won many blue ribbons.
> It's amazing how well
> You've jumped and you've ridden!
> You learned skills, you made pals,
> You've been a true champ,
> Which is why you just won . . .
> A scholarship to Juniper Ranch!
> XO,
> A Friend

OMG.
OMG.
OMGEEEEE.
I'm going to horse camp!!!!!!!!

CHAPTER FOUR

"I'M GOING TO HORSE CAMP!!!"

I squeal through my braces, gazing up at the carved wooden JUNIPER RANCH sign slung between two towering pine posts on the dusty road that leads into camp. A banner of colorful pennants flutters in the crisp Colorado air, welcoming me to what I'm pretty sure must be the most magical place on the entire planet.

"Whooee, kiddo, I think they could hear you on the other side of the mountain." My dad chuckles from behind the steering wheel of our car, which is rolling oh-so-slowly toward the grassy camper drop-off area.

"*What?*" my big sister Kay demands from the passenger seat, yanking out her AirPods and straightening her cat-eye glasses. "I don't know what you said because my ears just exploded and fell off my face."

"Sorry!" I chirp, turning my volume down to half-squeal. "It's just that . . . *we're finally at horse camp!!*"

"What gave it away?" Kay sniffs, punctuating her question with an overdramatic sneeze. "The smell of manure? Or the eau de barn sweat?"

"Maybe we should all focus on our own smells," my dad says, shooting Kay a look.

Though I can't quite see her face over the heap of gear that's piled around me in the backseat, I'm 99 percent sure she's rolling her eyes. My dad's driving Kay to engineering camp next, but she's clearly annoyed that she had to ride along for eight hours to my drop-off first.

"I'm allergic to farms!" she keeps reminding us.

"It's not a *farm*, Kay," I say, rolling my eyes right back at her. "It's an *elite* equestrian—"

"Own smells!" my dad interrupts. Then his voice softens, almost like he's saying a prayer to himself. *"Please."*

But not even a car squabble with Kay—who is sixteen, supersmart, and frequently "sensitive" (which is what my dad says we should call it, instead of "cranky" or "emotionally unhinged")—can slow my #HorseGirl roll today.

After someone at Oakwood secretly nominated me, I was awarded a full merit scholarship to Juniper Ranch "for exceptional riding ability and horsewomanship" *(eeep!)*, so my parents had no choice but to let me come to camp!

The muscles in my body coil with excitement, ready to spring from the car and bolt for the stable the moment we come to a complete stop. I *need* to find out which horse I'll be riding this summer.

According to Juniper Ranch's website—which I may or may not have memorized—the camp is home to more than fifty spectacular steeds, in every breed, size, and color known to man (or horse girl).

The FAQ (Frequently Asked Questions) page explains that no camper is allowed to bring along her own horse. Instead, we'll be paired up with one of Juniper's aforementioned spectacular steeds, based on our riding ability and personality.

(Do horses come in "awkward"? Asking for a friend.)

We're supposed to stay with the same horse for the entire summer so we can bond with our "halter-ego," as the website puts it. Which means there's a lot, *ahem*, riding on which horse I get assigned. It also means that someone at camp loves horse puns as much as me!

Beep-beep-ba-beep-beeeeep!

OMG. That's my dad.

He's honking a mortifying hello to the line of counselors, who are waving us toward a green clover field not far from a giant white barn. Dad rolls down his window and shouts, "Y'all accepting crazy horse girls??"

My dad thinks his jokes are *hilarious* . . . I think his

transition-lens sunglasses and HORSE DAD ON DUTY visor are similarly hilarious.

I slouch down in my seat as my cheeks burn hot-salsa red. "It's horse-crazy girls," I hiss. "Not the other way around."

But as my dad inches our SUV toward the drop-off spot, I slowly straighten up. I can't resist craning my neck to try to catch a glimpse of the Juniper Ranch horses through their half-open barn doors. Do I spy a giant Friesian?? *Whoa.*[1]

Then—above the sound of horses neighing and car doors slamming and campers shrieking with delight to be reunited—a sudden panic grips me.

In the flurry of finding the secret note and packing my trunk with my riding helmet and other essential gear (including about a dozen horse-girl T-shirts I bedazzled myself), I overlooked one VERY important detail: I've never been to sleepaway camp before. Let alone *horse* sleepaway camp.

My mind begins to panic-scroll through a list of potential catastrophes I forgot to consider:

---

[1] Friesians, like Clydesdales, have swishy "feathers" above their hooves and are known as supersmart, gentle giants. Friesians sometimes compete in dressage (a fancy sport where riders guide horses through teeny, tiny delicate dances), and they even carried knights into battle once upon a time. They're famous for their gloriously long, wavy manes and tails—they're like the hair models of horses!

WILLA'S FAQS
(FEARFULLY ASKED QUESTIONS)

What if I get the top bunk?
What if I get homesick?
What if I get poison ivy?
What if I get addicted to s'mores?
What if I have a bathroom emergency??
What if I drop my s'more during the campfire and everyone *assumes* I'm having a bathroom emergency???
Should I have packed more breeches?
Should I have packed more T-shirts?
Should I have packed a neckerchief??
What if the new girls don't like me?
What if the new boys don't like me??
What if the new horses don't like me???
What if *I* don't like me?!?!
WHAT IF I ROLL OFF THE TOP BUNK *AND* DROP MY S'MORE *AND* HAVE A BATHROOM EMERGENCY *AND* THERE'S NO INDOOR PLUMBING???

"Whoa," Kay says, interrupting the anxiety geyser that's exploding in my brain. "Your face is doing that stressy, crinkle thing again, like you really have to go to the bathroom."

"I don't!" I say, a bit too quickly.

"Calm down, Wills . . . It's just farm camp."

(I like to think this is my sister's way of saying, *It's going to be amazing, Willa. I love you.*)

"It's *horse* camp!"

(I hope my sister knows this is my way of saying, *Thanks, Kay. I love you, too.*)

Even though Kay and I argue a lot, she's always there when I *for real, for real* need her. (Like during a big horse show when my mom's on the other side of the world. Or a big horse-camp drop-off when my mom's on the other side of the world. Or Flag Day when—you get it.) Don't tell Kay, but I'm secretly going to miss her when she leaves for college next year. Like, a lot. It's just not going to be—

"You're gonna do great, Wills!" my dad booms. "Just look at you!"

My eyes flick down to the bedazzled T-shirt I made just for the first day of camp. In large sparkly rhinestones, it reads MANE CHARACTER ENERGY.

Just then, a counselor with glorious crimson hair and a neon-yellow traffic vest pops up beside my car window like a jack-in-the-box. She cheerfully but insistently motions for me to step out of the car.

I reluctantly surrender my phone to my dad. (The "Hoof Hints" section of the Juniper Ranch website made it abundantly clear that campers are not allowed to bring their "devices" to camp—under penalty of expulsion.) I take a deep breath, tug on the door handle, and step into the Colorado sunshine.

In the distance, a breathtaking ochre-colored stone ridge juts up from the earth, almost begging to be climbed (on horseback, obviously). Beyond that, a magnificent mountain peak pierces the blue sky, its head dusted with snow, its withers a meadow of lush greens and rambling wildflowers.

Whoa. I've got a feeling I'm not in Nebraska anymore.

My dad leaps out of the car, startling me from my reverie as he scoops me up into a giant bear hug.

(The "Hoof Hints" section of the Juniper Ranch website also made it abundantly clear that parents are not allowed to leave their vehicles during camp drop-off. But this does not stop my dad from leaping out of his vehicle during camp drop-off.)

"We're gonna miss you so dang much, Willa," he says, his voice cracking. "I want you to go out there and lasso up the best summer ever!"

I bite hard on my lip to keep from crying. (And also from correcting his horse metaphors—this isn't a dude ranch!)[2] But I can't help it . . . I feel salty tears forming in the back of my throat.

---

2   We're mostly focused on English riding at Camp Juniper, rather than the Western riding of a dude ranch. English riders use a smaller saddle and hold the horse's reins in both hands for more precise control. Western riders—like cowboys and cowgirls—hold the reins more loosely in one hand . . . to keep the other hand free for lassoing!

"Hey, hey—there's no crying at horse camp," my dad says, squeezing me tighter. I notice a few tears rolling down his cheek, too.

Kay swings open her car door and lurches out to join our family hug. If my mom were here, I know she'd be wrapping all of us in her arms, flashing her dimple-to-dimple smile and quoting some bittersweet Dolly Parton lyric about having the courage to spread your wings and fly high.

I wipe away the river of tears carving a milky trail through the sunscreen on my face and eventually untangle myself from the familiar limbs. I let out a shuddering sigh, willing myself to be brave. After we unload my mountain of gear, I shoo Kay and my dad back inside the car, then flash them two thumbs up.

"Don't worry, I got this!" I shout, more to convince myself than them.

That's when I notice that *everyone*—a long row of counselors, all the freshly arrived campers (including a handful of horse boys, *gah!*), and even a few stallions from the Juniper Ranch barn—has turned to stare at me. Oops. Guess I convinced myself a little too loudly.

Safety Vest flashes me two thumbs up and waves me closer. "Yeah, you *definitely* got this."

I bravely jog through the grass toward her . . . before realizing my giant trunk is looming directly in my path. But because I've already committed to running (and because *everyone* is watching), I skip forward faster to gain momentum, as if my trunk were a fence and I were a horse preparing to leap majestically over it.

Except—*eeeeek!*—just as I attempt to launch myself, my left foot catches in a hole in the ground. And—*aaaaah!*—I am now soaring sideways!

I hurtle horizontally through the air, like Supergirl stuck in landscape mode. By some miracle, my feet sail over the top of the trunk . . . by only a whisper. I hear a gasp go up in the crowd. But after a split second of soaring—*wheeeeeeeeeee!*—I lose altitude and tumble . . . *braces first!* . . . straight into the dirt.

Thud.

Welcome to horse camp!

CHAPTER FIVE

"Oof." A deep voice floats down from above. "The poor ground didn't see you coming."

"I'm fine, I fall all the time!" I hear myself saying. (It's true . . . but who brags about that to strangers??)

I pluck some dirt chunks out of my braces and shake a few pine needles from my braids, then notice the hand stretched in my direction.

I look up to see a pile of thick blond hair swooping messily above two emerald-green eyes above . . . a neckerchief. (Gah, I *knew* I should have packed one.)

"Welcome to horse camp," the boy says with a wink, tugging me to my feet. I notice he's *almost* as tall as me. "Guessing you're new?"

"I'm Wills!" (Great. As if I didn't just fall on my face in front of the entire camp, I am now answering simple questions with my own nickname.) "I mean—new! I mean, yes, I'm new. I mean—"

(Someone please stop me.)

"Cool," he laughs. "I'm Pasquale. I've been coming to Juniper since forever."

"Cool," I repeat, because I've suddenly forgotten every other word in the English language. As I stare at him blankly, I notice the bright blue WE ARE NEIGHHHHHVER GETTING BACK TOGETHER tee he's sporting beneath his neckerchief.

"Nice shirt," we both say at the same time. I glance down, remembering my own bejeweled top.

"Oh, thanks! I made it myself—"

Beeep, beep-ba-beep-beeeeep.

OMG. It's my dad. Honking goodbye (again) as he rolls slowly toward the camp exit. Maybe if I ignore him—

Beep beeeeeep!

"Don't forget to write us, kiddo!"

I realize my dad is not going to stop until I wave back, so I windmill my arm through the air in a half wave, pretending I'm simply adjusting my halo of braids. Before I can finish babbling about my skills with horse puns, rhinestones, and a glue gun, Pasquale takes a few steps backward and gives me a small salute.

"Gotta go claim the best bunk before someone else does. See ya around, Mane Character Energy!"

I give him an overly formal salute back (*why is nobody stopping me??*) as he spins on his heels and jogs away.

Fortunately, before I can shout anything else after him, Yellow Safety Vest bounces over to me and my gigantic trunk.

"Good on ya—ace landing!" she says (in what I *think* is a British accent?). The redheaded, rosy-cheeked counselor holds up her hand for a high five.

"Thank ya?" I say, the words slipping out in an awkward echo of her accent. After a beat, I remember, too late, to high-five her back.

Yellow Vest lets out a warm, throaty laugh. "You must be the famous Willa!"

"Guilty," I nod, wondering what magical powers she must possess to already know my name. (Did someone from Oakwood warn her about a girl who falls a lot?)

"I'm Nora, and I'm gonna be your counselor. Which is how I already know your name, love." She gives me a sly wink. "I'm originally from Australia, and I do a bit of stunt riding when I'm not at camp, and . . . crikey, listen to me prattle on! We'll get to all our fun facts later. For now, welcome to Juniper Ranch!"

"Pleased to meet ya!" I say. (Cringe.)

Nora is a gush of confidence and joy and brightness and beaded friendship bracelets (she has at least a dozen dangling from her wrists). She's exactly the kind of effortlessly cool #HorseGirl I want to be when I grow up. I vow to start working "crikey" into my vocabulary immediately.

"We'll be bunking in Misty—just over that hill." Nora nods ahead, toward a grove of trees.

According to the Juniper Ranch website, each of the camp's cabins is named after a famous horse book. I'm relieved that I've been assigned to Misty of Chincoteague with the older girls and not Pony Pals or Rainbow Dash with the baby riders.

While there are several #HorseGirl cabins (roughly organized by age and riding ability), there's only one #HorseBoy cabin. Which means my new pal, Pasquale, must be in King of the Wind. (Not that I'm thinking about where Pasquale's cabin is or what it's named, or which bunk he picked or whether he wears that neckerchief every day or just at camp or . . .)

"Most of the gals in your cabin have already checked in and are on a scout-about," Nora explains. "I've got to finish directing arrivals traffic, but you can drop off your trunk and get settled in. We'll meet back at Misty before the big riding test this afternoon."

Big riding . . . what?

Gulp.

CHAPTER SIX

Squeeeeeeeeeeeeeeak.

I push the cabin's rusty screen door open and peek inside. The scent of fresh cedar and bug spray and old riding boots floods my nose. Even though I've never been here, Misty smells familiar somehow . . . like coming home. (Or "home" if I lived in a *magical horse camp*—which I plan to suggest to my parents as our next move!)

The rustic timber cabin has been outfitted with three sets of bunk beds, tucked snugly against its side walls, along with one single cot (which I'm guessing must be for our counselor, Nora).

I spy a WASHROOM sign on a door at the back of the cabin and make a beeline for the bathroom. There's a sink with a faucet and—*kawooooosh!*—a toilet that flushes.

Phew. At least I can cross off indoor plumbing from my FAQ list!

I decide to unpack as quickly as possible so I can get to the stable and pick out my horse before they're all taken. My logical brain knows that there are plenty of mounts for all the campers. But my #HorseGirl heart is starting to panic that they might run out if I don't hurry.

After a swift scan of the room, I realize there's only one empty bunk remaining. And just as I feared . . . it's up top. *Womp-womp.* I guess now's as good a time as any to find out if I roll in my sleep as much as Clyde Lee!

I sling my sheets and comforter (which is emblazoned with the periodic table—thanks for the hand-me-down, Kay) up to the lofted bunk, climb the little wooden ladder with my daddy-longlegs legs, then attempt to make my bed with military precision.

As the daughter of an air force pilot, I am genetically required to make my bed every day. If I don't, I swear my mom will somehow find out from the other side of the world. She says if you do a good job on a small job every morning, you're showing the world you're ready to do a good job on the big jobs you'll face later in the day. (When I asked her how to show the world you don't feel like doing *any* jobs later in the day, she was *not* amused.)

As I struggle to tuck the sheets under the mattress (while I am sitting on said mattress), I bonk my head—and suddenly remember that I am "ouch" feet tall.

I battle the sheets for a bit longer, growing sweaty in the humid rafters of the cabin, until I finally surrender. (Please don't tell my mom!) Before I scurry back down the ladder, I quickly tape two photos to the back wall of my bunk: one of me and my family, and another of me, Clyde Lee, and all the Oakwood Flyers posing with their horses. Now this bunk *officially* feels like home!

Back on firm ground and with no time to waste, I fling open my trunk and dig out my riding boots. As I wrestle them onto my feet, I glance around the cabin one more time. And that's when I spot three familiar monogrammed trunks: *G*, *E*, and *N*.

Which means . . . Gwyneth, Everleigh, and Noel must also be in Misty! *Yesssssssss.*

I notice a thick copy of *The Horse Girl's Veterinary Handbook* on one of the bottom beds (that must be Gwyneth's spot). The top shelf of the next bunk is filled with a neat stack of mystery novels, along with a photo of Noel's horse from home, Ginger, wearing a Sherlock Holmes costume. The bed below that one is strewn with a mix of *Young Rider* and *Inside Gymnastics* magazines—all, naturally, addressed to Everleigh.

The third top bunk, however, is a bit more mysterious. There's a row of colorful crystals balanced on the bed frame, below a poster on the wall explaining "The 12 Horse Zodiac Signs." (I have no clue who's staying in that bunk, but now I know who to ask for Clyde's horoscope.)

But it's the bunk below mine that really causes my jaw to drop.

While everyone else's sleeping nook is pretty ramshackle—a mess of old comforters and sleeping bags—this one looks like it leapt off the glossy pages of *Barn Digest*. It's been expertly cloaked in a preppy pink-plaid duvet, with matching pink-plaid pillowcases, along with a pink-plaid throw pillow embroidered with the face of a regal horse.

A pink horseshoe blanket has been tossed artfully across the foot of the bed, while a string of pink horseshoe lights twinkles from the "roof" of the bunk, illuminating a dangling wreath of blue horse-show ribbons. Propped up on a little wooden shelf at the foot end of the nook are two elegant silver photo frames.

It's like a horse-girl Barbie Dreamhouse come to life!

I *think* I know who it must belong to . . . but the photos are all the way at the back of the bunk. So I can't be sure exactly who's smiling out from their frames.

And suddenly? I *need* to be sure.

I steal a glance back at the cabin door, then crawl gingerly on top of the plaid duvet. *Ahhhhh.* It feels as fluffy as a cloud of cotton candy . . . and somehow smells just as sweet. I'm momentarily distracted by the glowing horseshoes dangling above me. I consider closing my eyes, just for a second, after that long car ride . . .

Zzzzzzz—but no! I jolt myself awake. Must stay on track!

I lean in closer to the photo frames. The first reveals a girl with a smug expression, long glossy hair, and a prim blue riding blazer. She's sitting haughtily atop a gorgeous, leggy black Arabian with a white star on his blaze and a blue ribbon on his bridle . . .

It's Silver Streak! And Amara, of course. Just as I suspected.

I smile smugly to myself, mimicking Amara's expression in the photo. My sleuthing skills were correct once again. Which means . . . all the girls from Oakwood are in the same cabin! *Woo-hoo!*

But just as I begin to retreat from the bottom bunk, something in the second photo catches my eye. Amara is also front and center of this picture, one eyebrow arched coyly to the camera. Standing next to her, with one arm slung over her shoulder, is another figure . . . a boy. He looks strangely familiar. Where have I seen that face before??

I crawl closer to the silver frame to get a better look, when suddenly—*owww!*—my knee lands on something hard with sharp corners, not at all like the fluffy cotton candy I was expecting. I slip my hand beneath the duvet, feeling for what might be hiding below. I grasp something cold and sleek.

"Can I *help* you??" A sickly-sweet voice cuts through the stuffy cabin air.

Oh no. I'd know that voice anywhere.

"Amara?" I whisper, swiveling my head around. "I was just—"

But Amara has already swooped in next to me, snatching the phone from my hands.

"You were just *stealing* my personal property?" she asks, her piercing dark eyes narrowing. "Did you read my messages?"

"No! I was getting settled in and—"

"In *my* bunk??" she asks incredulously.

"No!" I say again.

Amara sweeps her palm across the bunk, as if to remind me that I am, indeed, currently sitting on her bed.

"Well, I mean, technically, yes?" I answer, hopping up from her bed, and (of course) bonking my head in the process. "But I was only there for a second. I got distracted by the absolutely beautiful photo of you and Silver Streak."

Maybe flattery will get me out of this?

"And also the, um, *beautiful* second photo of you with some other person I've never seen before," I stammer. "Or at least I don't think I've seen him before? I was just trying to take a closer look to see who it was."

"Why do you even *care* who it is?" she huffs. "It's like you're *obsessed* with me?"

"I was just trying to figure out who my bottom bunkmate is in case it turns out that I'm a sleep-drooler! And then my knee landed on—"

But Amara is no longer looking at me. She's furiously tapping into her phone.

"Actually, aren't we, um, not supposed to bring phones to camp?" I ask. And then immediately wish I could suck back the words.

Amara pauses for a moment, her eyes searching mine. Her lip snarls into a dangerous half smile.

"Do you realize you wouldn't even *be* here if it wasn't for me?"

My forehead crinkles in confusion.

"I mean, come on, Willa. There was no 'merit scholarship' to Juniper Ranch. My mom donated a bunch of money to the camp, and I *suggested* they create a scholarship so you'd stop whining about not getting to come."

I flinch—like someone just stabbed me in the heart.

"So if you want to *stay* here, I wouldn't tell anyone about the phone," she says, suddenly back to her sugary sweet singsong tone. "Or anything you might have seen on it?"

And that's when I realize. I didn't get into horse camp because of my "exceptional riding ability and horsewomanship." I got into horse camp because Amara felt sorry for me. And she's never, ever going to let me forget it.

"I'm not sure what's going on, Amara, but I swear I wasn't trying—"

"Exactly. You have *no* idea what's going on in my life," she hisses. "And now? I can't trust you at all."

The cozy cabin now feels stuffy and hot. The smell of roses wafting from Amara's bedding (did she bring designer pillow spray?) triggers a roiling wave of nausea deep in my stomach. The soft cashmere horseshoes on her fancy throw blanket begin to swim before my eyes. I clamp a clammy hand over my mouth.

No. No. Nooooo. I will not THROW UP ON AMARA'S BED!

"Howyagoin', campers?" booms a cheerful voice. "Looks like you two are hitting it off!"

Nora strides across the cabin with a clipboard in hand, her red curls bouncing behind her. She posts a barn chore calendar on the wall (with each of our names assigned to one day of the week), not noticing as Amara surreptitiously slips the phone into the back pocket of her pink breeches, untucking her shirt to cover the bulky rectangle.

"Wills!" shouts a chorus of familiar voices behind Nora. A wave of relief washes over me—and my urge to barf slowly subsides—as the Claremont triplets burst into the cabin and wrap me in a hug. I hug them back tightly, like my life depends on it.

"And I'm Clementine!"

A blur of purple hair whirls into the cabin behind Gwyneth, Everleigh, and Noel. The violet pixie cut is attached to a girl wearing a horse-shaped crystal on a lanyard around her neck. Our mysterious fifth bunkmate has arrived.

"Don't worry, I already saged the cabin for good horse energy," she assures me, pressing her hands together and bowing slightly.[1]

Amara crosses her arms and rolls her eyes. (Well, at least

---

[1] Saging (also known as smudging) is a purification ceremony using bundles of dried sage leaves to clean the air of bad energy or spirits. It's an ancient practice of many Indigenous cultures. Clementine learned to do it from her grandparents!

I'm not the only one in the cabin Amara clearly despises.)

"I think we'll need it," I reply to Clementine, forcing my lips into a small smile. (I'm not exactly sure what "saging" means, but I could definitely use some good horse energy right now.) "I'm Willa, but you can call me—"

"Wills." Clementine nods at me knowingly.

"All right, mates!" Nora announces. "We've got heaps of fun to get to—trail riding and creek swimming and mounted Camp Games at the very end of the session and—"

Clang-clang, clang-clang!

A loud bell rings in the distance.

"But first things first . . . It's time to meet your horses!"

CHAPTER SEVEN

"Circle up, campers," a gravelly voice calls out from the shadows of the barn.

Nora leads all of the Misty campers to the paddock beside Juniper's beautiful white stables. Gwyneth, Everleigh, Noel, Clem, and I stand on our tippy-toes, trying to catch a glimpse of the row of steeds that are happily swishing their tails behind us. The only one *not* vying for a peek at the horses is Amara, who appears to be focusing all of her energy on reapplying her eyebrow gloss.

Even though my stomach is still in knots, it's impossible to resist these beautiful creatures (the horses, not the eyebrows). I'm so enchanted with them—from their forelocks to their fetlocks—that I *almost* forget what just happened in the cabin with Amara.[1]

---

1   A forelock is the chunk of a horse's mane that falls between their ears onto their forehead (like bangs!), while fetlocks are the joints on a horse's legs just above their hooves.

I mean, it's super thoughtful and generous that she helped me get into Juniper Ranch, aka the most epic horse camp in the entire country . . . *if not the world?!*

But now I know my "merit scholarship" was totally fake. And that I probably don't truly belong here, unlike the rest of the girls in my cabin, who've been riding their whole lives. Even worse? Amara just oh-so-subtly threatened to take my scholarship away if I don't do every single thing she says all summer long . . .

"If you haven't met me before, I'm Mr. Gulch," the man—whose silvery hair peeks out from his dusty cowboy hat—says gruffly. "I happen to own this place. Now, I know you kids came to Juniper Ranch for a fun summer of riding. But if you want to *stay* here, you'll follow my rules. Otherwise, someone could get hurt. Or worse . . . make me grumpy. And I assure you . . . you won't like me when I'm grumpy."

Yikes. This is him *not* grumpy?

But Juniper's surly camp director doesn't look like he'd take kindly to questions at the moment, so I lock that thought firmly inside my brain. Even Amara subtly shoves her brow gloss back into her pink breeches pocket, brushes her silky hair from her eyes, and turns to face him.

"I have three rules, so they should be easy to remember," he continues. "Rule Number One: No riding alone, no riding after dark, no riding outside of Juniper Ranch trails."

I am itching to point out that Rule Number One is

actually three rules all by itself. But I wisely keep that math to myself.

"Oh sure, you'll get to wade into the creek on horseback, but that water is the edge of camp property. I don't want anybody crossing over to the other bank . . . or wandering around the Forsaken Forest." He pauses. "Just in case somebody decides to *un*forsake it."

A shiver runs down my spine. I remember seeing the Forsaken Forest on the Juniper Ranch map (which I may or may not have memorized on the ride to camp). It's a treacherously steep swatch of mountainside on the edge of camp, pierced with ghostly pine trees that have been singed black from a long-ago forest fire. Forsaken Forest has no proper trails. And no human inhabitants. It's marked with three red *X*'s on the map.

But I quickly shove my nerves aside. We're at a summer camp in the middle of the woods. *Of course* things are going to be a little, well, *forsaken* out here. Plus, we all have a Juniper Ranch map—who would be crazy enough to go off trail?

"Rule Number Two," Mr. Gulch continues. "Close the barn doors and stall doors behind you. We don't want any escapees. Remember: Check twice, worry once."

I repeat this phrase quietly under my breath. It reminds me of one of my Oakwood instructor Georgia's *brand-this-in-your-brain* rules, and I don't want to forget it. Mr. Gulch clears his throat over my mumbling.

"Rule Number Three: Safety first—no matter what. Never put yourself, your horse, or another rider at risk. I'm treating you all as responsible horse people. And I expect you all to live up to that responsibility. Do I have your word?"

He turns his unflinching stare down the line of Misty campers. One by one, we nod nervously back to him.

"Good," he growls, kicking a worn boot through the dirt. "Because if the rules get broken, y'all git goin'."

I have never been more afraid of a rhyme in my life. But then Mr. Gulch's lined face cracks into a smile.

"All right, enough scaredy-talk. Let's get y'all on some horses!"

The Claremont sisters let out a whoop, and Clementine forms a heart with her hands. Even Amara's eyes sparkle.

"Excuse me, Mr. Gulch?" I ask nervously. "What about our riding tests?"

Ugh, when will my FAQs stop leaping from my brain to my mouth??

"Oh, your horses'll be the riding test—they'll let you know if you passed or not," Mr. Gulch laughs. "But don't worry. I've already received reports from your riding instructors back home. So I know exactly which of my horses is the best fit for you right now. Well, at least for most of you . . ."

Most of us?? As he trails off mysteriously, I worry that Amara has already asked her mom to take back the money for my scholarship . . . and that Mr. Gulch is about to send me packing for home.

But instead, he reaches for the bridle of a midnight-black Arabian, coaxing the horse forward.

"Amara!" he calls out. "You're up."

Amara beams proudly—like she's won the horse lottery—and saunters over to the sleek steed, whose muscular shoulders make him look like he's spent time in the gym. The horse's eyes immediately lock with hers.

A weird sensation falls over me, almost like I'm experiencing *déjà horse*. Why does this all feel so familiar? And then it hits me: That's *Silver Streak*! I'd recognize his glossy black coat and white-star blaze anywhere.

"Hello, sweet boy," Amara coos, hurrying over to her steed. She strokes his inky black forelock, then traces the star on his muzzle. "Reunited at last! That must have been one long trailer ride from Nebraska."

She grabs one of the mounting blocks that Nora has set out along the paddock's fence, then swings a leg over effortlessly to mount Silver Streak. They glide slowly to the other side of the paddock in elegant, long strides. Even when they stop near the fence and Silver Streak shifts his weight impatiently onto his heels, they still manage to look—well—*magnificent*.

"Wait a minute," I whisper to Gwyneth. "Amara brought her own horse to camp? I thought that was against Juniper Ranch rules."

"It *is*," Gwyneth whispers back.

Everleigh does a side bend, leaning closer to my ear.

"Amara's parents made this big donation to camp. That's how they convinced Mr. Gulch to bend the rules and let her bring her own horse this year."

My eyes go wide. A big donation? So *my* scholarship was part of the reason Amara got to bring Silver Streak to camp?? *Crikey.* Maybe it wasn't so thoughtful and generous of her, after all . . .

"Silver Streak is *super* valuable," Gwyneth hisses under her breath. "I think he's worth more than our house!"

"He's, like, the Taylor Swift of horses!" Everleigh agrees.

"Yeah, and with Oakwood closing for the summer, Amara says her mom didn't want to leave Silver Streak in some random barn," Noel explains, nudging her glasses higher on her nose. "Where *anything* could happen."

Clementine now leans into our huddle. "Amara and Silver Streak must have an intense cosmic connection," she says earnestly. "I need to compare their astrological signs ASAP."

And that's when a lightbulb goes off in my brain. "Has anyone else noticed that Amara's been acting a little—"

"Did you folks have some kind of urgent question?" Mr. Gulch interrupts. "Or a bathroom emergency?"

"No!" I answer, far more loudly than I intend.

"Good," he says, adjusting the brim of his hat. "Because I hate being interrupted when I'm finding horses their people."

He strides over to the row of steeds, then pivots back to us. "*You*," he grunts.

I look around, confused about who he's pointing to.

"The one with the, uh, *interesting* shirt."

I glance down at my MANE CHARACTER ENERGY tee. Yep. I'm the camper, it's me.

Mr. Gulch leads a stunning chestnut Morgan to the center of the paddock.[2] The horse has four adorable white socks that stretch up to his fetlocks—sort of like he just trotted through a field of marshmallows. His flaxen mane and tail and fluffy bangs are blowing in the breeze—he looks like he's rocking an adorable blond Dolly Parton wig!

Suddenly, my eyes well up with tears. Maybe it's because Dolly Parton always reminds me of my mom. Maybe it's because of what Amara said in the cabin, reminding me that everything I've worked so hard for in the last year—from becoming a real horse girl to getting to go to a real horse camp—could be taken away in an instant. Just like all the times it has before, when my family's had to move and I've lost everything.

Or maybe it's because this steed is so freaking beautiful, I almost can't believe he's real!

"I hope you like fast getaways," Mr. Gulch says as I subtly wipe my eyes and turn off the feelings faucet in my mind. "Bandit's great-great-great-grandparents served in the cavalry once upon a time. He used to be a harness racer himself

---

[2] Morgans are one of the oldest horse breeds in the United States. Known for their courage and endurance, they served in the cavalry during the Civil War, carrying mounted troops in battle, scouting ahead for danger, and delivering important messages. Today, some of them still compete as harness racers, trotting or pacing as fast as they can while pulling a small, light cart (usually on two wheels) and a rider. *Wheeee!*

before he retired to Juniper Ranch. And he's still pretty quick on his feet."

I stare in silent awe at the magnificent creature before me, who has swiveled one ear in my direction, as if he's trying to decide what to make of me.

"Wait, you're sure this is *my* horse, Mr. Gulch?"

"What's the matter with Bandit? You're gonna hurt his feelings."

"Oh no, I *love* Bandit! He's beautiful. Like, the *most* beautiful horse I've ever seen. It's just, well, I'm still kind of a *novice* rider. And he seems like he's a professional?"

"What can I say?" Mr. Gulch says, handing me the reins. "The horse picked you."

And with that, the matter is settled. I have just been matched with the dreamiest summer-camp horse in the history of summer-camp horse dreams!

I gently rub my palm down his neck and shoulder. He lets out a sigh—oh, he likes it! I venture a scratch under his chin, and he nuzzles closer. So far, so good . . .

While Bandit and I get to know each other, Mr. Gulch matches the rest of the cabin with their summer steeds. Gwyneth, Everleigh, and Noel are paired with three stocky paints named Romeo, Sierra, and Tango—who happen to be siblings.[3] (They're not exactly triplets, but they look enough

---

3 A colorful and intelligent horse breed with quarter horse and thoroughbred bloodlines, paints boast distinctive white patches, like they've been splashed with—well—paint!

alike to confuse anyone who's not paying attention. The Claremont sisters can definitely relate!)

Clementine, meanwhile, walks directly to an older gray horse with a dusting of ivory dapples. Both she and the horse tilt their heads to the side in unison, almost as if they'd choreographed it.

"Is she mine?" Clem asks hopefully.

"Yes, ma'am," Mr. Gulch answers. "It's you and Aurora for the summer. How'd you guess?"

"We're on synchronous energy planes," Clementine says knowingly. "Plus? She's one of the only horses left!"

"Aha." Mr. Gulch lifts his brow and gives an impressed half grin, before passing over Aurora's reins to Clem. "Take good care of her. She's a senior."

"That's why she's so wise." Clem smiles. "Just like my horse back in California."

Mr. Gulch claps the dirt from his hands. "That should do it. You girls in Misty are all advanced riders, so after you double-check your saddles are secure, you can mount up and follow Nora out on the trail while I get the boys from King of the Wind settled."

(I can't help wondering which horse Pasquale will get assigned as his "halter-ego." Do horses have green eyes like his??)[4]

---

[4] Most horses have brown eyes; some have blue (usually pintos, paints, and Appaloosas), while a very few have light green (just like somebody else I know), gray, yellow, or even violet eyes.

As we all climb up on our mounts, Nora coaxes her own horse out from the stable. Immediately, our jaws drop.

Nora's steed looks like Black Beauty come to life. The magnificent black Friesian's long, wavy mane flows down past his shoulders—like he just got back from getting his hair crimped at the beauty parlor! He's showing off his new 'do with a glamorous, high-stepping trot, as if he's strutting down a fashion runway.

"Misty campers, meet Balthazar!" Nora announces proudly.

Right on cue, Balthazar bends his right leg in the air at the knee, leans back with his left leg pointing forward, then lowers his head to touch his muzzle to the ground in a dramatic, sweeping bow.

We all gasp. (Except for Amara, who seems to have missed the stunt and appears to be slipping something shiny out of her pocket.)

"Balthazar and I have a few tricks up our sleeves to show ya later." Nora grins. "For now, I think it's time for camp orientation. On horseback, of course!"

CHAPTER EIGHT

Click-click. Click-click.

Nora, perched comfortably in her saddle, softly clicks her tongue. Balthazar strides confidently forward, leading our little pack out of the paddock. Amara immediately steers Silver Streak to the front of the line (because of *course*), then Gwyneth and Romeo fall in, followed by me and Bandit, Clem and Aurora, Everleigh and Sierra, and—finally—Noel and Tango.

I sway happily atop Bandit as he strolls forward, holding his head high. He shakes out his lush golden mane and flicks his tail sassily, like he's onstage in front of thousands of adoring fans.

"You know you're a star, don't you, boy?" I ask with a giggle. He swishes his tail proudly.

As we set off down the main camp path, Nora points out all the VIPs (very important places) and VIHs (very important horses) of Juniper Ranch. I try to memorize every single detail. We're riding through the magical Horse Girl Land of my dreams, and I don't want to miss a thing!

"We've now arrived at the heart of Juniper Ranch," Nora says, pulling Balthazar to a stop in front of a sprawling wooden building painted cardinal red, with a large bronze bell in front of its entrance. "This is the mess hall, where we'll eat all our meals, and Big Ben, which Mr. Gulch rings for grub time or any other important events."

The mess hall is skirted by a wide, wraparound deck scattered with picnic tables, while billowing flags emblazoned with the names of famous horses and jockeys flutter from its rafters. Drool-worthy aromas—do I detect a hint of syrupy pancakes mixed with a note of last night's spaghetti and meatballs?—emanate from its doors as Bandit and I saunter past. *Mmmmmmm. My kind of fine dining.*

Nora then guides our horse parade past an outdoor fire pit surrounded by curved benches ("We'll be here tonight for First Fire—which is, naturally, the first campfire of the summer"), Mr. Gulch's office-slash-cabin ("Try not to bother him unless it's an emergency—I say this from experience"), and the infirmary ("We've got a nurse on staff 24/7, plus plenty of cots in case any camper is too sick, too homesick, or too *horsesick* to hunker down in their cabin").

"Horsesick?" Gwyneth asks with concern. "I'll have to look that up in the *HGVH* when we get back to the cabin." (Gwyn looks things up in *The Horse Girl's Veterinary Handbook* so often that she's given the book its own nickname.)

"Some folks really, really miss the four-legged friends they had to leave behind for the summer," Nora explains.

Gwyneth nods sympathetically, but I notice that I'm not the only rider who's glancing pointedly at Amara and Silver Streak. Amara, however, keeps her face forward, her back ramrod straight, and her smile perfectly smug, as if it's not *her* fault that nobody else got to bring their own horse to camp.

Nora and Balthazar walk on, continuing our sightseeing tour. She explains that all of the camp's cabins are nestled along a path leading uphill from the mess hall. The youngest riders' cabins—Pony Pals and Rainbow Dash—are at the bottom of the hill, followed by the intermediate-level Black

Beauty, then Misty, and finally, King of the Wind up at the top.

"Not because the boys are the most advanced riders," Nora explains. "We just think it's best to keep their dunny as far away from our noses as possible!"[1]

We all giggle—hygiene is *not* at the top of most horse boys' priority lists. (To be honest, hygiene is not really at the top of *my* priority list either. Who has time to shower when there are horses to ride?? But I keep that information to myself . . . and myself downwind of Amara.)

When we reach the end of the row of cabins, Nora loops around to another dusty dirt path. "Reckon we're ready for a trot?"

Click-click.

Before we can answer, Nora again flicks her tongue, and Balthazar dutifully picks up the pace to a trot.

Bandit, eager for speed and true to his harness-racing history, nudges ahead into Silver Streak's rump, trying to push past him toward Balthazar.

"Go right ahead?" Amara scoffs, pulling her steed to the side of the trail so Bandit and I can pass.

"Sorry!" I cry, but Bandit shoves ahead.

"Trot on!" Nora encourages us.

I hold my breath. It's always nerve-racking to shift gears

---

[1] "Dunny" is an Australian slang word for the bathroom. Fun fact: It comes from the British word "dunnekin," which roughly translates to "dung house."

for the first time on a new horse. But I let out my own *click-click* and give Bandit a light squeeze with my calves, just like I learned at Oakwood. He *clip-clop*s right into the one-two rhythm on the first try—sweet relief! His steps are full of swagger, like he's keeping time to a country song he knows by heart.[2]

Despite myself, a giant smile spills across my face. I guess I shouldn't be surprised that Bandit's good at following commands—he's the great-great-great-grandson of cavalry members, after all! I beam with pride as I realize that we both come from military families.

The other horses follow suit, trotting behind us. Amara and Silver Streak, however, end up in the back of the line. I can only imagine the sighs and eye rolls that must be rising from her like hot steam.

"Good on ya, everyone!" Nora points out a few more riding rings, a small hay barn, and a large swimming pool.

"That's about it for main camp," she says. "We don't have time to venture out on the horse trails today, but consider this a sneak peek."

Several arrow-shaped signs, slightly askew on little wooden posts, point to well-worn paths that wind into the surrounding forest and mountains. As we draw closer to

---

[2] Horses have four natural gaits, from slow to lickety-split: walk, trot, canter, gallop. For you drummers out there, walking is four beats, trotting is two beats, cantering is three beats, and galloping is four fast beats. It's my favorite music on the planet!

a trail marked JUNIPER CREEK RUN, the intoxicating scent of pine trees and adventure and animal sweat (and maybe *my* sweat?) floods my nostrils. I wish I could bottle it and wear it forever . . . Eau de Horse Camp!

Nora points over the steep trail edge, down to the creek flowing at the bottom of a series of switchbacks.

"Remember what Mr. Gulch said—always stay on the official trail and don't wander off into the Forsaken Forest," she says. "It's far too dangerous."

I gaze down at the groves of charred pine trees surrounding the trail. They stand guard like scorched scarecrows.

"And keep an eye out for mountain lions," Nora warns. "We've had a drought this summer, and they like to wet their whistles at our little creek."

"Mountain lions are among the only natural predators of horses," Gwyneth announces. "I read about it in the *HGVH*."

A shiver crawls up my back.

Nora glances at her watch. "Let's not dillydally, time to head back to the stable. We've got a lot on our plates this afternoon."

With that, she and Balthazar make a U-turn, shepherding us down the dusty main trail that leads back to camp.

"Plus humans," Clementine murmurs, as we follow behind.

"What's that, Clem?" I ask.

"Humans," she repeats. "They're horses' deadliest predators."

Chapter Nine

As we ride back toward camp, the crisp, crystal-clear Colorado air fills my lungs, and my worries seem to swirl away to the top of the pines. I'd forgotten how everything in life is easier to face when you're sitting on top of a horse. A girl could get used to—

Pfffffft!

Suddenly, Bandit stops short, skidding along the path and freezing in place. Oh no. Nora's warning about the mountain lions flashes in my mind. What is he seeing—or *smelling*—that I don't??

I quickly scan the ground ahead, searching for paw prints—or claw marks. But after I gaze more closely, I realize that the absolutely terrifying thing that's startled him is . . .

A pine cone.

A *tiny* pine cone. Ha!

"It's okay, Bandit." I giggle with relief. "I promise that little guy won't hurt you."

But to Bandit, the petite seedpod may as well be a baby mountain lion roaring at him. He shakes his blond mane furiously, as if to say, *No way am I taking another step closer, lady. Do you not see that scary, spiny monster ahead?*[1]

I let out another *click-click* and squeeze his ribs. But nope—Bandit has pulled the emergency brake and isn't going anywhere. Which means all the horses behind me are now forced to screech to a stop as well. *Blergh!*

"Um, Nora?" Amara asks from the back of the pileup, her voice as sugary and sour as a Sweetart. "It seems like Willa doesn't have control of her horse?"

I fire off a round of increasingly panicked *click-click*s at Bandit, but to no avail. He's now pawing the ground near the pine cone—and about to spook.

"Keep calm, Willa," Nora says evenly. "If he rears, lean forward, stay centered, and give him plenty of rein. You don't want him to topple back on top of you. In the meantime, try to sound super confident and reassuring."

---

[1] Horses have some of the largest eyes of any land mammals (including elephants) on the planet. Their peepers are eight times bigger than human eyeballs. But because horses' eyes are so far apart, they have a tricky time judging how far away (or how big) objects really are. They're also quick to notice movement and can startle at anything out of the ordinary. Which means they're especially nervous on narrow trails, where predators (or pine cones!) could jump out at them from the woods.

"And maybe less like a typewriter?" Amara oh-so-helpfully suggests.

"You've got this, buddy!" I say, trying to keep us both calm.

But Bandit's now tossing his mane.

Fortunately, Nora and Balthazar step in, sidling next to us. Nora reaches for Bandit's bridle and gently pulls him closer.

"Easy, big fella. Balthazar and I will show you it's safe," she says soothingly. Then she twirls Bandit around in place. "Turning him in a circle keeps his feet moving and shows him you've got a plan in mind, that you're the one in control."

After a moment, she coaxes Bandit a bit closer to the pine cone monster. Then away, then back, then away again.

"You want to get him used to whatever's spooking him. Eventually, he'll get bored by whatever it is and be ready to move on. Especially if you ride with intention—like you've got somewhere to be."

And Nora's right! After a few back-and-forths, Bandit marches forward (taking a *giant* step over the pine cone, just to be on the safe side), then happily falls into step right behind Balthazar.

"Excuse me??" Amara seethes, furious that Bandit and I have once again cut ahead of her. Silver Streak snorts his objection as well, shifting his weight impatiently.

Nora—ignoring the (literal) jockeying happening behind her—continues leading the way back to Misty.

"After we've tucked the horses at the stable, we've got to get ready for First Fire tonight," she says brightly. "But before that, you still need to pass your swim tests."

Groans and grumbles echo through the group. *Wasn't passing our horse tests enough for one day?*

"Ya know, if you don't pass your swim tests, you can't do the Horseback Swim in the creek later this week."

And suddenly? We're all ready to dive in!

Except for Amara . . . who insists she needs to return to the cabin first for a bathroom break. She tugs at Silver Streak, who seems reluctant to turn the way she's commanding him.

"Can't you go at the stable?" Noel suggests.

"It's an *emergency*?" Amara responds. *(Whoa, who would've thought Amara would have a bathroom emergency before I did??)* "I need to reapply my moisturizer, according to strict instructions from my dermatologist."

"All right, Amara," Nora sighs. "You can make a pit stop at the cabin and then meet us at the barn before we head to the pool. But I don't want you riding alone. Willa, you and Bandit go along with them."

BLERGH!

CHAPTER TEN

"It's not like I *asked* to come along for your bathroom break," I point out as Bandit and I clomp behind Amara and Silver Streak.

I can feel the annoyance radiating from her stiffened shoulders like the revolting stench rising from a pile of horse poo.

"Can you maybe stop talking about the bathroom?" she hisses, jerking Silver Streak's reins for a hard right into the woods that skirt the edge of camp, finding an opening near a clump of three quivering aspens.

"Okay, to change the subject . . . isn't this less of an *official* Juniper Ranch trail? And more like, um, the *Forsaken Forest*? Which Mr. Gulch told us we should, you know, absolutely, positively not wander into??"

"It's called a *shortcut*, Willa?" Amara slowly emphasizes

every syllable, as if she's speaking to a toddler. "There's a secret trail that cuts through the Forsaken Forest, then reconnects to the back side of all the cabins and the barn. Not even the counselors, or Mr. Gulch, know about it."

Silver Streak lifts his hooves gingerly, picking his way slowly through the pine-and-pebble-strewn trail. Which, if I'm being honest, I can't tell is a trail at all. It's just an overgrown sliver of dirt and rocks that's hard to keep track of beneath the bed of pine needles. I have literally no idea where we're going.

"So," I venture nervously. "How'd you find out about it?"

"From Pasquale." She shrugs, as if it's the most obvious answer in the world. "He's been coming here since forever."

And that's when it hits me . . . the boy in Amara's picture frame . . .

"You're friends with Pasquale?!"

Amara doesn't bother swiveling her head around to respond, but I realize it's a ridiculous question. She brought a framed photo of him to camp—*of course* they're friends. Or (gulp) *more than friends*??

It's definitely weird she never mentioned him before. But she's exactly the kind of girl who would have a secret, neckerchief-wearing boyfriend in every state. (I've never had *any* boyfriend, let alone one who lives across the border!) And—*OMG*—Pasquale's probably how she found out about Juniper Ranch in the first place . . . since he's been *coming here since forever*. And—*OMG again!*—that's probably another reason Amara's so mad at me. She saw me falling all over myself (literally) to talk to him at camp drop-off!

My cheeks burn hot at the memory of trading T-shirt-bedazzling tips with Pasquale.

"But the shortcut isn't on the camp map," I blurt, just to say something, *anything*, before my face bursts into flames.

"Did you miss the part about it being a *secret* shortcut?" She flips her head around, unable to resist flashing me an eye roll. "All the entrances are marked with three aspens planted in a triangle. It's really not that difficult??"

I wonder how Amara got Pasquale to tell her all of his camp secrets. But then I remember that *everyone* who meets Amara and her glossy hair wants to confess to her their deepest secrets, their highest hopes, and their darkest fears.

Including me.

"Amara, I'm *really* sorry I was snooping in your bunk and accidentally found your phone. I promise I won't tell anyone about it. And I'm so grateful that you convinced your mom to pay for my scholarship. It's one of the nicest things anyone's ever done for me. And also? I'm really, really sorry I tripped in front of Pasquale—I swear I wasn't trying to flirt with him!" After pouring out my guts, I take a deep breath. "I just don't understand what's going on—things seemed so great at Oakwood right before we got to camp. But now you've been acting so . . . *different*."

"Well, maybe I'm a different person at camp." She snaps

her head back to the front. "And maybe not everything's always about *you*, Willa? And BTW, you trip in front of *everyone*."

"I know! I just wanted to make sure you're—"

"I'm *fine*," she says, cutting me off. "And I *really* don't want to talk about my mom."

We walk on in silence for a few paces, until Bandit suddenly startles on the trail.

"Another scary pine cone, boy?" I ask soothingly, trying to keep him calm.

But when I glance up, I see something shadowy looming ahead, tucked around a bend in the secret trail and barely visible through the ghostly trees of Forsaken Forest. A pile of weathered gray planks leaning haphazardly against each other, like they might collapse if Bandit snorts at them the wrong way.

"Whoa, what's that?" I ask, pulling Bandit to a stop. I nod to the rotting collection of timber, which looks like it used to be a shack or a cabin once upon a time. Or perhaps home to the Wicked Witch of Forsaken Forest? I *knew* we shouldn't have broken Mr. Gulch's Number One Rule!

"I don't know," Amara breathes. Her tone is suddenly serious, and her eyes are (for once) *not* rolling.

We stare uneasily at the dilapidated, falling-down

structure. Its roof is carpeted with moss, and I can see right through some of its walls, whose planks dangle at unnatural angles, barely clinging together.

Caaaaaaaaaw!

A crow shrieks and swoops through a hole in the cabin, startling us all.

"I've never seen this . . . *thing* . . . in my life," Amara says nervously. "Maybe we lost the trail. Pasquale didn't say anything about a creepy cabin in the woods."

I glance over at Amara, unsure whether to believe her or not. But the chill in my spine is very, *very* real.

"Let's just get back to Misty," she eventually commands, clearly unnerved by this eerie detour.

After some tugging against a reluctant Bandit (*and* Silver Streak, I notice, who doesn't seem eager to turn around either), we manage to find our way back to the faint secret path and, eventually, to our cabin. We crosstie our horses to the front porch, then—*screeeeeech*—Amara tugs open the cabin's squeaky screen door.

"I'll be right back," she says, rushing straight for the bathroom, where she stays for several minutes, as I hop back and forth between my feet.

"I have to go, too!" I say when she finally emerges. (It's a fact of life that bathroom emergencies are contagious.)

"Fine," she huffs as if she, Queen of the #HorseGirls, should never have to wait on anyone else's biological functions. "I'll be outside with the horses. And, Willa?"

"Yes?" I ask, way too eagerly.

"Feel free to borrow some of my moisturizer."

My heart leaps at this cosmetic peace offering. Maybe Amara just needed some time and a secret trail ride to forgive me. My dad says sometimes people's emotions get the better of them and—

"Because you *really* need it."

Okay then, back to Peasant of the #HorseGirls.

I hustle through the cabin and slam the bathroom door behind me. *Phew—made it!*

As I'm washing my hands, I see Amara's luxurious face cream on the counter. I lift it to my nose and take a deep sniff. It smells like . . . *expensive*. But just as I'm about to dab a tiny smudge onto my face, I notice something else balanced on the counter.

Amara's cell phone.

I don't mean to look (I swear!), but the message notification is glowing bright. And I can't help seeing the preview of a text that pops up on the screen . . .

CHAPTER ELEVEN

An enchanting, smoky smell floats over the Juniper campers as we crowd onto curved wooden benches encircling a snapping campfire at the center of Juniper Ranch. (My hair is still a little damp from the swim test, which—spoiler alert—I passed!)

Fireflies dance in the woods behind us, and a horse whinnies contentedly in the distance. Nora and the other counselors pass around marshmallows, which we pierce ruthlessly with the spindly sticks we gathered earlier today after our trail ride.

We take turns twirling the sticky treats through the flames until their skins are crisped into a crackled mosaic. Then we rush back to our benches to smoosh them between layers of crumbling graham crackers and deliciously melty chocolate squares.

Or at least that's what Gwyneth, Everleigh, Noel,

Clementine, and I are doing. Amara, however, sits at the very end of Misty bench, stealthily slipping her phone out of her pocket and tapping away. I'm itching to ask the Claremont triplets if they know what Amara's mom's text means and why Amara seems so stressed about it. But I'm afraid that if I bring it up, she might literally throw me to the mountain lions.

I whip around to see if Nora's noticed Amara's secret scrolling. I know I promised I wouldn't say anything about the phone, but if *Nora* were to notice, maybe she could help Amara with whatever's going on?

Nora, however, is busy making her way to the front of the campfire, where a handheld microphone sits on a stand.

"G'day, campers!" Her voice echoes through the mic. "Welcome to First Fire—the first Juniper Ranch campfire of the season! Now that all the cabins are present and accounted for, and you've all got your marshmallows and chockie, who's ready for some ghorst stories?"[1]

A loud cheer goes up around the fire pit. I glance around, confused. At first I think "ghorst" must mean some kind of exotic Australian s'mores topping—just like "chockie." But then Nora helpfully explains that ghorst stories are ghost stories about horses.

In other words, 🐎 + 👻 = 🐴💀

I join the campfire cheer with my own tentative

---

 1   Chockie is delicious Australian slang for chocolate.

yelp—somewhere between terrified and thrilled. I'm relieved to be sitting next to Clementine, who's wearing her horse-crystal necklace, which she promises will protect our entire cabin, no matter how spine-chilling the stories get.

Fortunately, the first few tales told by the other counselors aren't very scary at all—in fact, they're pretty hilarious. There's one called "The Ghorst of Frankensteed" and another named "The Telltale Hoof" and then comes "An American Rear-Wolf in Paris," about a horse who turns into a wolf in France and is constantly rearing up to howl at the moon.

As the stories get more and more ridiculous, I giggle happily with the rest of the girls from Misty. (Except for Amara, who keeps checking her pocket.)

I glance around again to see if anyone else has caught the telltale glow from her phone when I notice Pasquale (eeep!) guffawing on a bench with the boys from King of the Wind. He's pawing his hands in the air and howling as if he were the aforementioned Rear-Wolf in Paris.

"Ugh," Amara says. "He's *so* annoying."

A wave of jealousy rushes over me. Amara already knows Pasquale well enough to be annoyed by him? That proves it: They *must* be in a relationship! *Blergh!*

"So how long have you and Pasquale—" I start to ask. But a gravelly voice interrupts me.

"All right, all right. Those make-believe stories were okay." Mr. Gulch has made his way to the microphone at the front of the campfire. "But I've got a real one for ya."

The sun begins to slip lower in the sky, and a cool breeze tumbles down from the mountains, ruffling my T-shirt.

"In fact, it's about a real horse. Who used to live right here at Juniper Ranch."

The giggling and guffawing die down. All the campers lean forward. Mr. Gulch seems scarier now than he did when he was telling us about the camp rules. (And I did *not* think that was possible!)

"This horse's name was Marley. He belonged to Juniper Ranch's owner before me. He was an old horse, a good horse, *loved* kids riding him. He was a cremello, white as a sheet with icy blue eyes. Heck, he looked a lot like a ghost even when he was alive."[2]

Mr. Gulch pauses for a moment, letting his words roll across the rows of campers like an eerie fog.

"But Marley had a bad habit. He liked to wander through the Forsaken Forest, across the creek, and into the neighboring ranch. Just couldn't get enough of the clover over there. Juniper ranch hands had to keep an eye on old Marley, I'm told. The next-door neighbor didn't take too kindly to a horse munching in his field. In fact, he warned Marley's owner that if he caught that horse on his property one more time . . . well. He left it at that. But they caught his drift. Then one summer night . . . Marley vanished. Poof. Gone."

---

[2] Cremello horses have a special gene that gives them creamy coats, white manes and tails, and icy blue eyes.

Mr. Gulch snaps his fingers, and we all startle. I feel a mix of eagerness and dread, like when I'm watching a scary movie and cover my eyes but then can't resist peeking through my fingers.

"Old Marley seemed to have simply disappeared. Except for a few days later . . . when a ranch hound found his long white tail—neatly braided and dangling from the branch of a pine tree, just across the creek."

Mr. Gulch pauses for a moment. And I gulp. Loudly.

"Now, some say it was mountain lions that got old Marley. Some say it was the owner of the ranch next door. Some say it was a gang of horse thieves who wanted a rare cremello and chopped off his tail to mark exactly which horse to steal in the night. But others say—and I'm not sayin' I'm one of 'em—that it was a human ghost from the Forsaken Forest . . . who wanted his very own horse to ride."

A shiver of fear runs down my back, like a finger sliding down a row of piano keys.

"Whatever happened, Marley was gone. And to this day, whenever Juniper Ranch campers ride past Forsaken Forest . . . they feel it. You might feel it, too. A chill in the air. Maybe your horse startling out of the blue. They say that's because Marley's still there. He's still searching for his lost tail . . . and that delicious clover . . . and perhaps . . . a new rider from the living."

The camp falls into a frightened silence, as Mr. Gulch's words hang in the air.

Heeeeeeeeeiiiiiiii!

A beastly squeal pierces through the quiet. It's coming from the edge of the forest, just behind the campfire! I jump in the air and let out a startled scream, along with almost everyone in camp.

Ahhhhh!!!!

Panic races through my body, and my eyes go wide as I scan the forest for a hulking white figure—what I'm sure must be the Ghost of Marley. Then we hear the sound again . . .

Heeeeeeeeeiiiiiiii!

CHAPTER TWELVE

"Hahahahahaaaaa!"

A group of boys jump out from behind the trees, doubled over in laughter.

"You should have seen your faces!" Owen, the tallest one, snickers. He twirls a strange, hand-carved whistle on a lanyard, then raises it to his lips.

Heeeeeeeeeiiiiiiii!

It sounds, of course, exactly like an eerie ghost-horse screech. The boys cackle and convulse, clapping hands over each other's backs.

"That *wasn't* funny," Amara hisses.

"You're right," Owen replies apologetically, his lips bending into a contrite frown. But then he bursts into another cackle. "It was *hilarious*!"

Amara unleashes an epic eye roll and spins on her heels.

My eyes, meanwhile, search the pile of horse boys, looking

for one neckerchief in particular. And then—suddenly—his dazzling green eyes meet mine. Pasquale shrugs and sheepishly brushes his hair from his face, as if to say, *I swear, Willa, I had nothing to do with this. I'm so sorry. I'd never hurt you.*

Or at least that's what I'd like to imagine he's trying to say. In reality, it's probably more like, *Ugh, I got some chockie in my eyes! Now I can't stop blinking!*

"I think that's just about enough excitement for one night," Nora says briskly, rising from her bench. She cocks a disapproving eyebrow at Griff, the goofy, ginger-haired counselor in charge of the King of the Wind boys. "I'll deal with you lot later. Misty campers, time to head home for lights-out!"

We dutifully obey, following Nora as she sets off up the cabin path. But I catch her stealing a quick backward glance at Griff and the boys, who are still cackling their heads off. And as she flips her crimson curls around, I see the tiniest hint of a grin on the corner of her lips.

Screeeeeeeeech.

Nora flings open the squeaky screen door. We trudge up the worn wooden steps and drag ourselves back inside Misty.

"I was *really* scared," Noel whispers. I realize she's close to tears.

"I still am!" I squeak (partly to make Noel feel better and mostly because it's true).

"There's literally *zero* reason to be scared?" Amara asks-slash-answers, clearly riled. "It was just the *Peasants* of the Wind Cabin trying to frighten us, which for some reason, boys around the world think is, like, their full-time job? I mean, even Mr. Gulch, with his ridiculous 'Casper the Friendly Ghorst' story!"

"It's *Marley*," Everleigh corrects her.

"You're *Marley*!" Amara snaps back. (Whoa. Is Amara so worked up that she's actually running out of creative insults?)

"You looked a little afraid yourself," Gwyneth points out. Amara scrunches her nose. But I notice she doesn't disagree.

"Now I'm never going to fall asleep," Noel whimpers.

"Talk about literal night-*mares*," I agree. (Dang it, if only I had a blank T-shirt and some glitter right now!)

"I'll give you a horse crystal to help, Noey," Clementine says reassuringly, rummaging through her trunk to find the perfect polished pony.

"Blimey, that sure got a little spine-tingling at the end."[1] Nora comforts us as if she's trying to soothe a horse that's spooked. "And I'm sure Mr. Gulch will have a word or two with Griff about controlling his campers."

---

[1] "Blimey"—like "crikey" or "golly"—is an Australian expression for surprise or an *aha!* moment. Allow me to use it in a sentence: *Blimey, you're tall for a girl!*

She looks off dreamily for a moment, before quickly snapping back into focus.

"Ahem . . . but remember that the First Fire stories are all in good fun. We have a big day of riding ahead of us tomorrow. Balthazar and I are going to teach you some super-cool tricks, then we'll discuss the big end-of-camp Horse Games. So let's all get ready for bed and dream of happy riding in the morning!"

After some nudging (and yawning) from Nora, we brush our teeth and climb into our bunks, settling in for the night.

Amara makes a big show of tugging on her eye mask and earplugs, but I'm pretty sure I can see the glow of a phone light streaming up from the bottom bunk. Clementine, meanwhile, passes Noel a tiny horse figurine to slip under her pillow and protect her from nightmares. Everleigh gracefully somersaults into her bunk, while Gwyneth tucks *The Horse Girl's Veterinary Handbook* into bed beside her, just in case she wakes up and needs a midnight diagnosis.

As for me? I snuggle under Kay's periodic table blanket. *Aaaaaaah.* Who knew the elements could be so cozy?

Then, with a click, Nora flicks off the light. And we all, eventually, drift off to sleep.

Zzzzzzzzzzzz.

Chapter Thirteen

Gasp!

I'm rumbled awake by the sound of a stampeding elephant. Wow, if Extreme Snoring were an Olympic sport, Nora would have just won the gold medal. I tug an entire row of noble gases over my face and try desperately to fall back asleep.[1] But the blast of Nora's honks keeps me staring into the black hole of my periodic table blanket. Eventually, I toss it away and look around the room—shocked to find the other Misty campers still sleeping soundly.

Ugh. Maybe a sip of water will help me drift off? I swing my legs to the end of the bunk and lower myself quietly down the ladder, taking care not to wake Amara. Fortunately, she's tucked peacefully beneath a sea of pink blankets, with only a pile of her perfectly glossy dark hair peeking out.

---

[1] Noble gases are natural gases that are grouped together on the periodic table, just like on Kay's blanket. (Not to be confused with Bandit's natural gases!)

I tiptoe toward the bathroom. And that's when I hear a whinny—a *real* one this time—coming from the barn. It sounds exactly like Bandit! Or maybe Aurora? Or it could be Tango. Or . . . *what if it's the spirit of Marley coming to take Bandit to the Forsaken Forest?!?!*

I know it sounds crazy to believe in a ghorst story. But just because the horse boys were trying to scare us doesn't mean it's not true. Especially after Amara and I discovered that creepy cabin today. What better place for a horse-thieving spirit to hide out, waiting for unsuspecting ponies? (And/or . . . *their riders*??)

I realize the only way I'll ever fall back asleep in a million years is if I check on the horses in the barn to make sure they're safe.

But after taking a few steps toward the cabin door, I stop myself. *What the haaaay am I doing??*

I've already broken part of Mr. Gulch's Number One Rule today, by following Amara down the secret path into the Forsaken Forest. And now I'm about to break the rest of it??

I'm only here on a scholarship—and a fake one, at that! I can't risk getting kicked out of horse camp before it's even begun.

Besides, if I so much as *breathe* on the cabin's screen door, it will squawk louder than Nora's snores. Not only will I wake up everyone in Misty, but I'll have to explain exactly why I'm sneaking out in the middle of the night to search for an imaginary demon horse that may or may not be haunting the barn!

So that settles it. I'm going straight back to bed. Immediately. The end.

I stare at the cabin ceiling above my bunk, Mr. Gulch's words echoing in my mind: *No riding alone, no riding after dark, no riding outside of Juniper Ranch trails.* My brain can't stop searching for a loophole—like a tongue that can't resist wiggling a loose tooth.

And then it occurs to me . . .

If I slip out of the cabin, I won't *technically* be riding alone, riding after dark, or riding outside of Juniper Ranch. I'll just be taking a little stroll. On my own two feet. To the barn. Which is *inside* Juniper Ranch.

Loophole unlocked!!

Another whinny rings out from the barn. Bandit is obviously calling for help. And I don't have time to debate my own brain any longer.

I plunge down the bunk ladder and tiptoe to my trunk, silently opening its lid to fish out the flashlight Dad forced me to pack. (Please don't tell him he was right about the whole "trust-me-Willa-you'll-need-a-flashlight" thing.)

Then I scamper to the bathroom to borrow a bit of Amara's super-fancy face cream . . . just like she suggested.

I work quickly, slathering the expensive lotion all over the hinge of the cabin's screen door. Holding my breath, I gingerly unlatch the handle, willing it not to squeak or creak as I oh-so-slowly push it open.

Phew—sweet silence. (Wow, this stuff actually works . . . Maybe I actually *should* take my skin care more seriously!)

I slink outside, where I am immediately hit with a blast of chilly mountain air. My body, clad only in flannel pj's, shivers in the moonlight.

That's when I decide that taking the (dark! scary!) secret shortcut between the cabin and the barn really wouldn't be so bad after all . . . if it helps me get to the horses (and the warm barn) faster.

I move swiftly, using the flashlight to find the triangle of slender aspens that mark the entrance to the secret path . . . and the Forsaken Forest. I try to distract myself from the sinister trees by imagining I'm Everleigh at a gymnastics meet—leaping oh-so-delicately over the pine needles crackling (*shhhhhh*) beneath my toes.

After a few twists and turns, I finally see it: the warm yellow glow of the light above the barn door. *I'm soooo* close.

But there's no forest to camouflage me in the wide field surrounding the stable. So I make a mad dash for the barn doors, gasping for breath as I unlatch them and fling myself inside.

Phew—I'm in! I slump back against the large wooden doors, allowing myself a brief moment to exhale.

But I know it won't be long before Mr. Gulch makes his midnight barn checks. So after I catch my breath, I make a beeline for Bandit, sweeping my flashlight across the open top half of his stall door to make sure he's safe and sound.

Oh no. *Oh no.* There's no sign of my beloved halter-ego. *Did the Ghost of Marley get here before I did??*

I gather my courage, inching my body closer and closer to the stall as the flashlight trembles in my hand. I perch on my tiptoes to peek over his stall door. My heart pounds—terrified of what I might find below.

Pfffffffffft.

Oh. It's Bandit. On the floor. Snoozing happily in his pile of straw.[2]

I exhale sharply, then snort at my own ridiculousness. To think I actually believed a ghorst had stolen my horse! "Sweet dreams, Bandit," I whisper.

But just as I'm tiptoeing back out of the barn, a loud *neigggggghhhh* rings out from Silver Streak's stall. Ugh, I probably woke him up with all my ghorst-hunting.

I scurry over to investigate, promising myself that it's only for a moment, just to make sure he's settled in for the night. But as I lift my flashlight toward his stall door, the shaft of light is blocked by a dark figure looming in the shadows.

---

[2] It's just a rumor that horses only sleep standing up. While equines *can* snooze upright, they also need to lie down each day for deep sleep. (Same!) Fun fact: Most grown-up horses only sleep between three and five hours in total each day, although younger foals need more *zzzzzz*'s.

"Ahhhhhh!" I scream.

"Ahhhhhh!" a deep voice screams back.

I jolt the flashlight in its direction. The shaky beam eventually lands on the terrifying neckerchief of . . .

"Pasquale?!" I nearly faint with relief. "What are *you* doing here?"

"I was about to ask you the same thing!" he says with a laugh, wiping his palms on his jeans.

"I was checking on Silver Streak," we both blurt, then laugh again. (Thank goodness it's dark in this barn, because I am once again blushing. The same shade as Amara's Barbie-pink bedding.)

"I couldn't sleep, then I heard a loud whinny." Pasquale shoves his hands in his pockets and looks up at me sheepishly. "After that ghost—*ghorst*—story, I guess I'm a little on edge."

"Me too," I confess.

I glance around to make sure there are no supernatural equines lurking behind us in the stall. But all is as it should be: Silver Streak's saddle is tucked into its monogrammed cover, resting on a rack just outside his stall (where Amara insists on keeping it, rather than in the tack room with all the other saddles) and his hay net is heaping full.

"After I checked on Alfredo"—*OMG, Pasquale's halter-ego is named after my favorite pasta?!*—"I thought I'd swing by to give Silver Streak a NickerDoodle. My sister likes to spoil him with fancy snacks."

"I'm super picky about my snacks, too!" I say, way too eagerly. Then my forehead wrinkles in confusion.

"Wait, your *sister*? Silver Streak belongs to Amara."

"Um, yeah?" He chuckles. "Amara's my sister."

Whaaaaaat? My brain nearly explodes with relief. Still, I feel the need to clarify. "So you're *not* her secret boyfriend?"

"Um, no!" He bursts into laughter. "I'm technically her *step*brother. My mom married Amara's dad a while ago. Amara and I don't see each other very often. I live with my dad in Colorado, and she lives in Nebraska with her mom. But this summer they decided Amara should come to the same horse camp I've been going to since forever. They said it would be good for us to have 'sibling bonding' time or whatever."

My mind continues to spin. *Amara has a stepbrother? Who ALSO loves horses?? And lives in Colorado with his dad and an extensive collection of neckerchiefs???*

"Cool," I finally say, because I can't decide which of the ten thousand questions racing through my mind to actually ask Pasquale. So I turn to Silver Streak instead.

"You weren't scared, were you, boy?" I ask, stroking his white star. He nickers back happily, cutting some of the tension in the stall. I'm still tongue-tied from "Amara has a brother and it's Pasquale" shock, so I look around for inspiration.

I search the stable for *anything* to discuss instead of this.

My eyes land on a heart, traced in the dirt of the barn aisle, just outside the stall.

"Oh wow, did you draw that?" I ask, pointing at the dirt. (Really smooth, Willa!)

"Draw wha—"

"Hello?" a gruff voice calls from outside of the barn. "Everybody safe and sound for the night?"

"It's Mr. Gulch!" I panic-whisper, diving back into the stall and ducking low, half hiding beside Silver Streak.

Pasquale lifts a finger to his lips and points to the back door of the stall, which opens directly to the paddock outside.

"We can go that way, one at a time," he whispers. "Mr. Gulch will only walk down the front aisle of the barn. It's just his regular nightly check of the horses—he won't suspect anything if we slip out the back through the paddock."

I nod nervously, agreeing to this plan because my mind has gone entirely blank for a second time tonight—and I am now in *very real* fear of getting kicked out of horse camp.

"I'll go first to make sure there are no counselors nearby," he whispers urgently, opening the bottom half of the Dutch door and motioning for me to crawl outside behind him. "Count to ten, Willa. If I whistle by then, you're in the clear—run for it!"

OMG, Pasquale remembered my name? And he's going first to make sure I don't get in trouble?? He's like my knight in—

"Count to ten, Wills!" he hisses.

"Okay!" I hiss back. I begin silently mouthing the numbers as he slips away into the darkness.

"And . . . ten!" I whisper proudly to myself.

I wait for a beat. And then another beat. And . . . *um* . . . where's the whistle? Where . . . is . . . *the whistle*?! Pasquale and I didn't discuss what I'm supposed to do if there's no—

Pheeeeeeew-iiiiit.

Phew. I close my eyes, exhaling in relief. And then remember the second half of Pasquale's instructions . . . RUN FOR IT!

I duck down and scramble out the little opening in the back of Silver Streak's stall, stumbling my way through the paddock muck. Eventually, I slip through the paddock gate and dash back down the secret path, trying to ignore the menacing appendages dangling above me.

"You're just branches!" I blurt, attempting to scare the scorched timbers before they reach out and snatch me—as one does when sprinting through a haunted forest.

When I finally reach Misty, I pad up the porch steps, gasping for breath. I carefully lift the screen-door latch, praying to the #HorseGods for a squeak-free open.

And—*phew*—Amara's lotion once again does the trick.

As I step inside the cabin, I'm greeted by the magical sound of Nora's elephant snores. I've never been so happy to hear mouth breathing in my entire life!

I silently climb into my bunk, hunker down under the

periodic table, and attempt to slow my racing breath and swirling mind. I try to think calming thoughts of horses and s'mores and, um . . . *neckerchiefs.*

But visions of scary trees and Amara's furious face and terrifying pine cone monsters overtake my brain. *Ughhhh.* I'm never going to be able to fall . . .

Zzzzzzzzzzzzzzz.

CHAPTER FOURTEEN

"Ahhhhhhh!!!"

I bolt awake from a deep slumber, startled by a bloodcurdling scream. It's still early—a frosty chill hangs in the mountain air and goose bumps cover my arms—and I'm not sure if I'm still dreaming (or night-*mare*-ing) or not.

I quickly glance around the room. Clementine and the Claremont triplets have also shot up in their bunks, confused and groggy. I lean forward from the edge of my bed, craning my head upside down to check on Amara.

But her pink palace is empty.

"That scream sounds like it's coming from the barn." Nora leaps up from her bed and dashes toward the cabin door. I clamber down from my bunk and quickly follow her, along with Gwyneth, Everleigh, Noel, and Clementine, who are already clomping ahead. We race—still in our wrinkled pajamas and hastily tugged-on boots—out the screen door, toward the sound of the wailing.

Nora leads the charge, bursting through the barn doors and rushing down the aisle. But we all freeze when the voice cries out again.

"He's *gooooone!*"

I look up to see Amara standing alone in Silver Streak's stall.

She's right—there's no horse in sight. Only a pile of straw in the corner . . . and an open box of NickerDoodles.

My heart skips faster. *Those are the same NickerDoodles Pasquale was feeding Silver Streak last night.*

Amara's shoulders heave as she covers her face with her hands. Tears begin to streak her cheeks. I have never, ever seen Amara—Queen of the #HorseGirls—cry. Which means this is really, truly, *absolutely* happening. *Oh no, oh no, oh nooooooooo.*

As difficult as Amara can be sometimes, I know down deep she has a giant heart. And if there's one thing she loves most in this world (other than her eyebrow gloss and her HorseTube followers), it's Silver Streak. That horse is her entire world.

"Tell us what happened, love?" Nora steps into the stall and wraps a tender arm around Amara.

"I have no idea," Amara sputters between dramatic sobs. "I came in early this morning to make sure he was settling in okay. But then? When I got to his stall? He was *gooooone!*"

As her wailing winds up to an even higher pitch, Mr. Gulch rumbles toward us.

"That horse was here when I did my barn checks last night. Everyone was present and accounted for."

Just then, a strong breeze whooshes through the barn, rustling a blanket that's draped over the paddock door at the back of Silver Streak's stall. Suddenly—*bang!*—the door swings open, slamming against the outdoor wall.

"The paddock door wasn't latched!" Mr. Gulch hollers, snatching the blanket away to reveal an open exit behind us. He then stomps outside into the dirt. "And the paddock gate's wide open!"

A jolt of panic pulses through me. *The paddock gate.* Which Pasquale and I escaped through last night . . .

"But I closed it," I say, then clap a hand over my mouth.

Everyone spins around to stare at me.

"What do you mean, you closed it?" Mr. Gulch snarls, as every eye in the barn bores into me.

I gulp.

"Last night. I . . . I couldn't sleep. I heard whinnying coming from the barn. It sounded like a horse was worried, or sick, or . . . I don't know . . . being attacked by a ghorst? Anyway, I decided to come by to check on Bandit."

"Last night?" Nora protests. "But I would have heard you leaving the cabin."

I consider explaining to Nora that no living creature on

earth could have heard anything above the sound of her sawing logs. But I (wisely) decide that now is not the moment for hard truths.

"It wasn't very late?" I fudge. "I wanted to make sure the horses were safe. Everyone was A-OK, just like Mr. Gulch said! So I decided to leave through the paddock. To, um . . ."

Ugh. How am I going to explain this part??

"To uh . . . avoid waking up . . . any of the other horses," I stammer.

"But what were you doing in *Silver Streak's* stall?" Amara demands, her eyes narrowing.

"I was checking on him!" I mewl. "I swear, Amara. He was right here, safe and sound."

I drop my head to my chest, certain that those will be the final words I utter at horse camp. I probably just admitted to breaking at least five gazillion of Mr. Gulch's rules. And I'm absolutely, positively, 100 percent sure he's going to send me on the next bus home.

But to my surprise, Mr. Gulch doesn't tell me to pack my trunk. Instead, he kneels to the ground just outside the paddock door.

"Can't tell if these hoofprints are fresh," he mutters. "At least two dozen horses probably came in and out of the paddock yesterday."

"I'm sure I closed the stall door *and* the gate behind me, Mr. Gulch," I say desperately.

"You check twice?" He tilts his head up at me.

"I . . . I . . ." I gulp again. Did I check twice?? *Blergh, now I can't remember!* A thick cloud of doubt rolls through my brain. "I think so?"

"You *think* so?" Amara huffs. She points a finger at me. "Isn't it obvious? *Willa* was the last one here. And now Silver Streak is gone!"

"Amara, I would never," I blubber. "I mean . . . we're friends!"

"We *were* friends," she says, her voice icy. "It's called past tense?"

Ooof. I've never actually been wounded by grammar before.

This is probably the moment I should point out that Pasquale—her own stepbrother—was *also* in Silver Streak's stall. In fact, he was there before I was. And the whole "let's slip out through the paddock" plan was *his* idea. And also?? He maybe, possibly (probably not) drew a heart in the dirt for me!

But instead? I say nothing. I'm not sure if I'm protecting Pasquale or myself. But I decide it doesn't matter.

Because in the end, Amara is right. This *is* all my fault. If only I'd remembered Mr. Gulch's rule—check twice, worry once—I wouldn't be worrying times infinity right now. I'd be 100 percent sure I closed the stall door *and* the paddock gate. Silver Streak would be safe in the barn right now, noshing on some NickerDoodles.

And I wouldn't feel, once again, like the worst #HorseGirl in the world.

"That's enough," Mr. Gulch interrupts. (At first I think he's trying to give my brain a pep talk, then I notice he's looking pointedly at Amara.)

"Let's start with the assumption that no Juniper Ranch rider would ever do anything to intentionally harm a horse. If anything, this was an unfortunate *mistake*. And we're here to learn from our mistakes, correct?"

Amara blinks innocently at him, but Mr. Gulch is now looking directly at me. I try not to cry as I nod back to him. Then I steal a glance at Amara, hoping I can convey just how terrible I feel. But she refuses to meet my eyes.

"Seems to me that Silver Streak decided to take himself on a little vacation," Mr. Gulch continues. "But horses almost always cut their great escapes short when it's feeding time. He'll be back by suppertime—I'd bet my hat on it."

Then, almost to himself, he adds, "Unless he decided to join that pack of wild mustangs that moved through the ranch this spring . . ."

All of our eyes go wide—especially Amara's. I have no idea if Mr. Gulch is joking or not. (It's impossible to tell with his Resting Frown Face.) But I'm praying we don't find out.

"I read a story about a real horse in Utah who ran away with a pack of mustangs and didn't return for *eight* years," Clementine murmurs.[1]

Ugh, I guess Mr. Gulch was *not* joking.

---

[1] A few years ago, a horse named Mongo really did run away with a pack of wild mustangs in Utah. He returned to his owner eight years later. *Phew!*

"If for some reason Silver isn't back by tomorrow—" he continues.

"Silver *Streak*," Amara sniffles. "He prefers his full name."

"I'll head out to search the neighboring ranches." Mr. Gulch stands up and claps the dirt from his hands. "But let me make one thing clear."

We look up at him nervously.

"Absolutely *no* campers are to go looking for that horse. If I catch a single one of you wandering off camp property, *everyone* will be sent home. Horse camp will be over. Finished. Done. *Finito. Completo.* Got it?"

We all quickly nod our heads. "That's *real* Taurus-rising energy coming out," Clementine whispers.

"Good," Mr. Gulch grunts. "For now, we're all going to continue with our lessons and activities, just like normal. Silver Streak will be back in no time."

Nora gives him a reassuring nod. She guides the still-snuffling Amara and the rest of us back toward the barn's front door.

"One more thing," Mr. Gulch calls after us, clearing his throat. "There's no need to tell the other cabins or contact your parents about any of this. The grown-ups have the situation under control. If you worry the younger riders or your family back home, you'll just cause a panic for no reason."

"But, Mr. Gulch!" Amara says with alarm. "My parents

will absolutely want to know if anything's happened to Silver Streak. He's *extremely* valuable."

"*Nothing* has happened to Silver Streak," Mr. Gulch replies sternly. "So give me twenty-four hours to find him. Juniper Ranch is in enough trouble as it is."

CHAPTER FIFTEEN

"*Enough trouble as it is?* What did Mr. Gulch mean by that?" I whisper to Gwyneth.

We're back at the stable after changing into our bright red Juniper Ranch long-sleeve tees. Despite the morning's panic, Nora insisted we participate in Camp T-Shirt Day, just like everything was normal—which it absolutely is *not*.

"I think Juniper Ranch may be running out of money," Gwyneth whispers back. "Amara's mom said Mr. Gulch might have to sell—"

Nora heaves a saddle my way, interrupting our conversation.

"You heard what Gulch said. We're gonna keep calm and carry on. So let's mount up, ladies!" Nora's voice is overly cheerful. She's obviously trying to distract us.

"Who am I supposed to ride?" Amara sniffs as she snaps on her pink helmet. "Since my horse has been *stolen*?"

Amara has cut the sleeves off her Juniper Ranch tee so that it's now an oh-so-chic tank top—and, of course—*waaaay* cuter than the normal, boring, long-sleeve shirts the rest of us are wearing. (I'm suddenly desperate to dash back to the cabin and snip the sleeves off all of my shirts, too!)

"No one nicked Silver Streak," Nora replies firmly.

"At least that we know of," Noel adds quietly, as Amara lets out a loud huff.

"For now, you can ride Macaroni."

"The *pony*??"

"Yes, the strong and talented pony!" Nora smiles. "It's good to get riding experience on horses of all sizes. You'd be amazed at how many riding tricks I first learned on a pony."

"Speaking of which?" Amara says, in her treacherous uptalk. "I thought you were this big-deal movie stunt rider? It's *so* nice that you're taking a time-out to work at a camp for a bunch of kids."

A tense silence fills the air. Amara is clearly tailspinning.

But Nora responds cheerfully, not letting on if she's bothered by the implication that she flunked out of Hollywood. "Top-notch question! Balthazar had a hard landing on our last picture. The vet says he's all healed up, but I thought I'd ease him back into work before we start our next film. Just to make sure he's one hundred percent ready for his close-up."

Balthazar lets out an offended *pfffffffffft*, as if to say, *I am 200 percent ready for my close-up!*

"Mr. Gulch gave me my first job, so I always come back when he needs me. And right now . . ." Nora's voice trails off.

Hmmm. That's the second time this morning someone's mentioned trouble at Juniper Ranch. I make a note to ask Gwyneth what's really going on when we're back at the cabin.

"Blimey, I should recruit Macaroni for my next movie!" Nora says, changing the subject as she strokes the pony's forelock.

"Ugh, it's like we're stuck in an Outback Steakhouse commercial," Amara mutters. She's clearly annoyed that she couldn't get a rise out of Nora, so she's now shifted gears to mocking her Aussie slang.

Clementine gently points out that Australian English *is* in fact, English, and that all languages evolve through slang, adding to the rich diversity of our planet. But Amara's not done with her tantrum.

"*I* should get to ride Bandit! *I'm* the one who's suffering! Willa should have to take Macaroni. It's *her* fault Silver Streak is gone."

"Amara," Nora says sharply.

Then Noel jumps in, shoving her glasses higher on her face. "You're being really disrespectful—to Nora and to Wills."

"And to Macaroni!" Everleigh adds, pointing to the sorrel pony.[1]

---

[1] Horses (or ponies!) with copper-red coats plus manes and tails the same shade or lighter are often called sorrels (which is a shade of chestnut). Think of them as the gingers of the horse world.

"We know you're upset that he's missing," Gwyneth adds gently. "But we're your friends, Amara. We'd never do anything to hurt you on purpose."

Amara glances around at us, then looks at the ground like she's trying to decide whether to tell us something. Her mouth trembles. But then she stops herself, steeling her lips into a furious line. "You have no idea what it's like to lose your horse!"

"You can take Bandit," I say quietly, stretching his reins toward Amara. "I don't mind."

She juts her chin in the air and gives me a tiny nod, as if she's a princess granting a favor to a lowly subject, then takes a step toward my steed. But Nora holds up her hand like a stop sign.

"Willa, you will ride Bandit so that you continue to bond and become mates—it's one of the guiding principles of Juniper Ranch."

"I should be bonding with Silver Streak right now," Amara snaps. "He's *my* mate!"

But Nora ignores her. Instead, she gives me a leg up to mount Bandit. He nickers happily as I heave my daddy-longlegs leg over his saddle.

"Amara," Nora says, finally turning to her. "You'll ride Macaroni for today, and we'll find another solution tomorrow."

"Fine. I'll take the stupid pony," she grumbles. "My

parents will *love* hearing about this when I'm finally allowed to call them."

I bite my lip, knowing that Amara could 100 percent call her mom anytime she likes with her contraband phone. And make sure horse camp is finished, done, *finito, completo*—for all of us.

CHAPTER SIXTEEN

"Today's lesson will be a bit different than what you're used to," Nora announces. She's led us all the way back to Juniper Creek Run, at the edge of camp. "Instead of groundwork or jumping over rails in the arena, I'm going to teach you some cross-country riding skills.[1] We'll blaze over real fences and logs and streams—like you might do on a *real* wilderness adventure."

Despite how truly awful this morning was, a thrill of excitement shoots through me.

I've never really ridden outside an official ring before (besides our brief camp tour yesterday and, yes, my Grand Theft Equine in the Oakwood parking lot back home with Clyde). The trail feels so much more . . . *alive*. Like anything could happen.

---

1 Groundwork exercises take place while riders are—*welp*—firmly on the ground! (Instead of on top of a saddle.) Groundwork is an important way to practice skills and build trust with your steed.

Nora begins by explaining some basics of trail riding in the mountains.

"Remember, your horse doesn't want to fall any more than you do." She leads the way atop Balthazar as the rest of us follow behind on our steeds. "It's all about balance and trust. When you're heading uphill, you'll want to lean forward. When you're headed downhill, lean back. Trust your horse to find his footing.

"It's truly incredible how resilient and adaptable horses are," she continues. "They find a way to embrace the moment. Instead of worrying about the loose rocks—or, ahem, *pine cones*—that gave them a little scare yesterday, they're focused entirely on the next step in front of them."

Ugh, I wish *I* could focus entirely on the next step in front of me. But unfortunately, all I can think about is how I'm going to be forever known in Juniper Ranch lore as "The Girl Who Let a Horse Escape and Ruined Camp." *Crikey.*

"Ouch!" Amara yelps from the rear of our parade of horses as Macaroni carries her far too close to a low-hanging pine branch, which scrapes across the bare skin of her shoulder. "It's like he's doing it on purpose!"

"He probably just had an itch he wanted to scratch," Nora calls back from the front of the line. "Next time, keep the sleeves!"

Gwyneth swivels her head back toward me and gives me a little wink. Despite myself, I have to bite my lip to keep from giggling.

As we round a bend in the trail near the top of a steep incline, the sound of galloping hooves thunders toward us. My heart leaps—it has to be Silver Streak!

But when the pine trees on either side of us give way to an open clearing at the top of the hill, there's no sleek black Arabian waiting for us. Instead, it's a dark brown quarter horse turned out in Western gear, ridden by Mr. Gulch.[2]

"Any luck?" Nora asks. The cheerful lilt in her voice has descended into quiet worry—the way grown-ups sound when they're talking to each other about serious business, as if the rest of us couldn't hear them.

"Nothing so far," he says, his lips cemented in a grim line. "But we've still got some daylight. Before the mountain lions come out again."

Nora nods. And I suddenly realize why she took us on the trail ride today. She was hoping we'd stumble upon Silver Streak.

"Wait . . . the mountain lion thing is actually true??" Amara asks, fear lapping at her voice.

"I'll be back at camp by chow time with an update," Mr. Gulch says. He lets out a brisk *click-click*, tugging the reins gently across his horse's neck to spin him around, then heads back down a trail toward the neighboring ranch.

"Don't worry, Amara," Gwyneth says consolingly. "Mr. Gulch will find him."

---

[2] As previously mentioned, Juniper Ranch focuses on English riding, but Mr. Gulch prefers to ride Western—like the cowboy he is.

Then she turns back to me and whispers, "And as soon as Silver Streak turns up, I'm sure Amara will go back to her normal self."

"Is that supposed to reassure me?" I whisper back, and she grins.

"I swear, Gwyn," I continue. "I closed that gate. At least I'm ninety-nine percent sure I did."

"Of course you did, Wills," she nods.

But I can't quite tell if she believes me. And honestly? I'm not sure if I even believe myself anymore.

I'm dying to tell Gwyneth about Pasquale, but I'm terrified that if Amara finds out I was hanging out with her brother in the barn, things will only get worse. (Times infinity!) And I'm dying to ask Pasquale about the stall door and the paddock gate, but Mr. Gulch just forbade us from discussing Silver Streak with anyone outside of Misty. Plus, Pasquale left before me—he won't have any idea if I remembered to close the gate or not. *Blergh!*

Despite our deflated spirits, Nora insists we finish our ride. And soon the fresh mountain air fills my lungs with a cool calmness. Bandit is a champion on the trail today, marching fearlessly up and down the steep mountain switchbacks, adapting to the shifting terrain, and even leaping over a fallen pine log with ease. I guess it's nowhere near as scary as a pine cone!

When we reach a clearing, Nora instructs us all to dismount. Then, as soon as we're down from our horses, she commands us to mount up again.

"But we don't have any mounting blocks." Noel gestures to the wilderness around us.

"That's right, mate!" Nora's eyes dance with excitement. "So what happens if you're out in the woods without a mounting block or a pal to give you a boost?"

"You, um, walk home on your own two feet, being sure to stay safely on the marked trail?" Noel suggests as we all giggle.

"Ah, but what if you've got a very long ways to go?" Nora inquires. "You're all strong horsewomen. Now I want you to learn some survival skills, so that if you ever end up alone in the woods, you can save yourself."

She points to one of her friendship bracelets. Its beads spell out a single word: "GRIT."

"It means having the courage and determination to do something—even when it's really, *really* hard. Even if you have to find another way."

I listen to her keenly, wishing I had my own magical pile of grit.

"I'm going to teach you one of my favorite riding tricks," Nora continues. "It's called a running mount. Also known as a vault."

"I love vaults!" Everleigh squeals. "Do we get to use a springboard, like in gymnastics?"

"Nope!" Nora smiles. "No springboard, no mounting block, no boost. You'll be able to get back up on your horse all by your lonesome."

Our eyes all go wide with wonder. Nora passes Balthazar's reins to Amara, then asks if she can borrow Macaroni for the demonstration. "It's much easier to learn on a pony."

"Be my guest," Amara says icily. "I've already lost one horse today. You might as well take this one, too."

"Very generous of you, Amara!" Nora tilts her head in a little bow, then guides Macaroni to the center of the clearing, standing on his left side.

"You want to grab a handful of mane and the reins with your left hand, then plop your right hand on his saddle. The saddle will take the brunt of your pulling action, so make sure the girth is secure.[3] And never, ever tug on the reins while you're mounting, or it'll pull on the bit and hurt the pony. Once you've checked that you're all set, it's time to start moving!"

And then—as if Macaroni can read her mind—he begins walking, then trotting, as Nora jogs thrillingly along beside him.

"Now it's time to *juuuuuuuump*!" She hops into the air, pushing off with her left foot, then flinging her right leg all the way over Macaroni's saddle.

---

[3] A girth is a strap that goes under the barrel of a horse to keep your saddle in place, kind of like a belt. Once your horse is tacked up, check to make sure the girth is tight but not *too* tight; you should be able to fit a few fingers between the strap and your horse's belly, all the way around.

It's like watching a champion horse jumping a fence—except the fence is a horse and the horse is Nora's body!

"And we're up! Easy breezy." Nora finds the stirrups with her feet and picks up the slack in the reins. "Now who wants to give it a whirl? All of Juniper Ranch's horses have been trained in running mounts, but Macaroni makes for an ace teacher."

I exchange nervous looks with the other girls. And then, before I know what's happening, my gangly arm shoots into the air above my helmet.

"That's the girl!" Nora winks as she vaults down from Macaroni and brings him to my side.

My palms grow clammy as I hand Bandit's reins to Gwyneth and walk toward Macaroni in the center of the ring.

"That's it, stand on his left side, then grab a handful of mane and keep the reins loose," Nora encourages me.

I try to remember all the steps Nora just taught us, but they swirl in my mind. Do I hop on my left foot and grab the saddle with my right hand? Or leap with my right hand and then snag the saddle with my left foot? *Gah, how did she make this Twister game look so easy?* Before I can mentally untangle my limbs, Macaroni starts walking—and then trotting!

Ahhhhhhh!!!

I skip along beside him, clinging to his mane and trying to keep up. But he's so much faster than I imagined.

"Juuuuuuuuump!" Nora cries.

"I'm *tryiiiiiiing!*" I cry back.

When I finally get airborne—*wheeeee!*—Macaroni's saddle is already several strides ahead of me. So when I *juuuuuuuuuump* . . . I land on a pile of thin air.

Thud.

"I'm okay!" I quickly shout, tasting the muck that's now seasoning my braces.

"That's a relief," Nora says, waiting for me to catch my breath before she breaks into a grin. "Cuz you're goin' again!"

Oooooof.

I slowly pick myself up—plucking the pine needles from the arms of my camp shirt (thank you, sleeves!)—and walk back over to Macaroni. But before I make my second attempt, Nora wriggles off her GRIT bracelet and hands it to me.

I look at it dubiously. "Because I fell in the dirt?"

"Nah, mate," she says softly. "Because you got back up."

As I slip the bracelet around my wrist, Nora's words about finding the courage to do something—even when it's really, *really* hard, even if you have to find another way—echo in my brain.

Maybe instead of feeling terrible about Amara's horse disappearing and wallowing in it's-probably-all-my-fault guilt, I need to show a little more . . . grit?

And figure out a way to find Silver Streak myself.

CHAPTER SEVENTEEN

Slam.

The screen door bangs behind us as we file back into Misty after our ride for "rest hour." It's like we're kindergartners being forced into nap time, but I'm not complaining. It'll give me time to come up with a plan to find Silver Streak. And recover from my *multiple* attempts at a running (or in my case, *falling!*) mount. And stop my tummy from rumbling like a stampede.

I tug off my riding boots, grab a sack lunch that Nora kindly had delivered to our cabin (*yummmm*), and climb up the ladder to my bunk.

As I do, I notice Amara has already pulled her pink blanket over her head. A soft glow creeps out from its delicate edges. She must be on her phone again. Which, of course, reminds me of the message I saw from her mom. She seemed desperate to talk to Amara about something important . . . something about insurance. Whatever it was, it clearly couldn't wait until after camp. But after Amara's temper tantrum earlier today? I value my life way too much to ask.

Instead, I hoist myself over the bunk ladder, flop onto my bed, and dig through the crinkly paper-bag lunch. Along with sandwiches shaped like ponies, there are "hay bale" Rice Krispies treats for dessert (aka, every #HorseGirl's dream meal).

As I crunch loudly on my sticky hay bale, I notice the rest of the cabin has gone eerily quiet. (If only snacks came with silent mode.) I guess the realization that Silver Streak might be really, truly lost—or *worse*—has begun to settle in.

I gobble down my pony sammie, lick my fingers, then slide a notebook from the shelf at the end of my bunk. I swiftly get to work, compiling a list of every suspect who could have been involved with Silver Streak's disappearance (whether accidentally or super on purpose).

SILVER STREAK SUSPECT LIST
WILLA (ME!)
WILD MUSTANGS
MOUNTAIN LIONS
SCARY HORSE THIEVES
GWYNETH
EVERLEIGH
NOEL
CLEMENTINE
AMARA
PASQUALE
NORA
MR. GULCH
THE GHOST OF MARLEY

I decide to evaluate each of the suspects, one species at a time.

First up are the wild mustangs. Mr. Gulch may have been joking about tame horses running away with a herd, but according to Clementine, it can happen! Maybe Silver Streak just needed a break from Amara and some "me time" with his fellow steeds??

Then there are the mountain lions. As Gwyneth pointed out, they're natural predators of horses. And there are plenty of them roaming in Colorado—they've even been known to attack horses if they're desperate for food. *Ugh*, I'll never, ever in a million years be able to forgive myself if something like that happened to Silver Streak.

Which brings me to horses' other natural predators: humans.

Technically anyone at Juniper Ranch Camp could have snuck out last night and led Silver Streak into the forest. But Mr. Gulch warned us not to tell any of the other cabins. So I begin, naturally, with Misty.

I've been friends with the Claremont sisters long enough to assume they don't have a side hustle as tweenage horse thieves. But they *do* know exactly how valuable Silver Streak is. And even though they're my "mates" (as Nora would say), I still have to consider them.

Clementine seems nice enough, but none of us had ever met her before a few days ago. She's the one who pointed out that humans are natural predators of horses. *And* she seems to have psychic powers (or at least powerful pony crystals). Could she actually make a horse disappear??

Then there's Amara's stepbrother, Pasquale. He was right next to me last night in Silver Streak's stall, bringing him NickerDoodles. Could he have been trying to sneak off with his new sister's horse in a jealous rage when I interrupted him? I'll have to watch him carefully. (Eeep!)

Next up? The grown-ups.

Mr. Gulch said something about Juniper Ranch having "enough trouble as it is." Gwyneth told me the camp is having money problems. Then Nora mentioned she came back because Mr. Gulch "needed her." Silver Streak is *extremely* valuable—Noel said he's the Taylor Swift of horses. Maybe Mr. Gulch made it look like Silver Streak went missing so he could secretly sell him? And then use the money to save the camp?

Or what about Nora? Maybe she needs a new stunt horse to train for her movie career? She said Balthazar was all healed from his fall, but what if that's not true? Silver Streak is a champion rider and a real-life *Black Beauty* . . . He'd be an instant hit on the big screen!

It looks like the only name I can *actually* cross off the list is Amara. She was truly terrified when Mr. Gulch mentioned the mountain lions earlier today, plus she loves Silver Streak more than anything. (Including her eyebrows!) She'd never do anything to hurt her heart-horse.

Other than that? I don't think I can eliminate anybody else. Including myself. Or Marley!

I know I shouldn't believe a silly ghorst story that Mr. Gulch probably made up to keep us from sneaking out of our cabins at night. (Oops?) But on the other hand? Silver Streak *did* disappear the exact night we heard that scary story . . . and not far from where Marley went missing all those years ago.

Coincidence?

I have no idea!

For now, all I've got is my suspect list . . . and a hunch of just where to start looking.

Chapter Eighteen

"I volunteer for barn chores!" I shoot my arm in the air, thunking the cabin roof in the process. "That way Amara doesn't have to do them."

It's the best plan I could come up with to get back to the barn after rest hour without raising any suspicions. And if I can suck up to Amara in the process? Double win.

A loud huff bursts from the bunk beneath mine. Amara's making it abundantly clear that a few measly barn chores can't possibly make up for my crime of (*allegedly!*) leaving Silver Streak's stall door and the paddock gate open.

"Fine," she sighs. "Since I'm *obviously* not up for shoveling manure after all I've been through today?"

Nora sucks a breath through her teeth, then reluctantly nods. "Go on, Wills. Just be back before the dinner bell."

I stash my suspect list in my breeches pocket, then scamper down from my bunk, pull on my boots, and dash out the cabin door. If I'm going to find out what happened to Silver Streak, I'd better start at the scene of the crime.

"Hello?" I call out tentatively when I reach the barn.

Fortunately, the only reply is a few whinnies. Mr. Gulch and the stable hands must still be searching for Silver Streak, while the boys from King of the Wind must still be out on their afternoon trail ride with Griff. I'm all alone except for the horses.

But I know I have to move quickly. I still have to muck out the Misty camper stalls, solve a horsenapping, and get back to the cabin—all before dinner!

I hoof it to Silver Streak's stall first. It's still heartbreakingly empty, of course. Even the pile of hay that was here this morning seems to be gone. And the spilled box of NickerDoodles, too.

Poor Silver Streak—he's used to being treated like a king. With elaborate grooming, glamorous tail braiding, and even custom snacks (aka my dream life). Now he's probably lost in the woods—*or worse*—all by himself, with no treats or massages or attention or fancy braids. He must be so scared. And hangry.

That's when something clicks in my brain. Something so obvious I can't believe I didn't think of it before.

Why would Silver Streak's hay net be empty?? And why

would his box of NickerDoodles be missing??

Amara was with me the entire day, either on the trail or in the cabin, so I know she didn't have time to come by the barn and tidy up his stall. And all of the Juniper Ranch stable hands are out searching with Mr. Gulch.

I guess it's *possible* that one of the counselors or a kid from another cabin cleaned up the stall while we were out on the trail ride. But something isn't adding up. Why would anyone move Silver Streak's food? Unless . . . unless . . .

Unless that someone assumed he wouldn't be coming back.

I feel my spine stiffen. My eyes scan his stall again, more desperately. Something else feels wrong, but I can't put my finger on it. What am I missing? *Think, Willa!*

I step inside the little wooden room and slowly spin around. That's when I notice it, just outside the stall door. Silver Streak's saddle rack . . . it's empty!

GASP.

Which means someone must have moved Silver Streak's saddle. Or . . . put it on to ride him.

DOUBLE GASP!

OMG. OMG. OMGeeeee. This is *proof* that whatever happened to Silver Streak wasn't an accident. That beautiful horse didn't just wander away through the paddock door . . . Someone was *riding* him!

It's also proof that Silver Streak probably wasn't horsenapped by a ghost. (Ghosts don't need saddles, right??)

And he definitely wasn't taken by mountain lions. Mountain lions don't mount up when they're planning a sneak attack. And neither do wild mustangs! (They are *firmly* against saddles, in fact.)

Most importantly, the missing saddle means . . . *drumroll, please* . . . I am no longer a suspect!!!! Because I know for certain that *I* did not take Silver Streak. Or his saddle!

I tug out my suspect list and quickly update it—crossing my own name off with a great flourish.

SILVER STREAK SUSPECT LIST
- ~~WILLA (ME!)~~
- ~~WILD MUSTANGS~~
- ~~MOUNTAIN LIONS~~
- SCARY HORSE THIEVES
- GWYNETH
- EVERLEIGH
- NOEL
- CLEMENTINE
- ~~AMARA~~
- PASQUALE
- NORA
- MR. GULCH
- THE GHOST OF MARLEY **

**Call me superstitious, but I can't quite bring myself to cross off Marley's name yet. What if ghorsts *do* need saddles?

I cram the crumpled page back in my breeches pocket and return to my barn chores. I hurry over to Bandit, cross-tying him outside his stall. Then I step back inside, dragging along my handy-dandy shovel, pitchfork, and wheelbarrow. Bandit helpfully "supervises" by peeking his head through the door and snorting loudly.

"Okay, okay, I'll work faster!" I giggle, sorting the horse droppings from the straw and shoveling the yucky stuff into a wheelbarrow to cart away, before sprinkling fresh straw all around the ground.

Honestly, I don't even mind all the pooper-scoopering. The repetitive motion of shoveling helps calm my spinning brain.

Plus, it gives me one-on-one time with Bandit and the other horses. My spirit always seems to lift just being around them . . . like they're my own personal helium tanks!

When I finally finish mucking every stall, I make sure each Misty horse is tucked in safe and sound. I check and (yep) *double-check* to make sure all of their doors (both the barn aisle side and the paddock side) are firmly latched. No more escapees on my watch!

After I finish my muck-a-palooza, I balance the shovel outside Bandit's stall door and pull the suspect list from my pocket to look through it once more before I return to the cabin.

But just as I do, a brood of booming voices echoes from the front of the barn. The King of the Wind campers must be back early from their ride.

I quickly fold the notebook page and start to stuff it back in my pocket when a shadow falls across the slip of paper.

"Mane Character Energy!"

"Oh, haaaaay!" I say, startled. "I didn't realize you were . . . here."

"I ride faster than those jokers—gotta stay at the front of the pack." Pasquale grins, then his emerald green eyes dart down, landing on my suspect list. "Whatcha workin' on?"

"Homework!" I answer, sounding slightly deranged. "I mean . . . it was, uh, just my list of barn chores? But I'm all done now."

I crumple the now-sweaty page into a ball before Pasquale can get a closer look. I vividly remember Mr. Gulch's warning not to tell *anyone* in the other cabins that Silver Streak is missing. (Even if said *anyone* is wearing a new red neckerchief that perfectly matches his camp T-shirt . . . *Swoon.*)

Pasquale beams his sparkling gaze straight into my eyes, holding it there for a long beat, as if he's trying to decide something.

But as his lips part to speak, a jumble of rowdy boys rush around him.

Clang-clang! Clang-clang!

Chapter Nineteen

Clang-clang! Clang-clang!

Big Ben, the camp bell, is reminding everyone it's dinnertime. Which means my conversation with Pasquale will have to wait. I dash from the barn back to Misty as fast as my feet will carry me. But, *ugh*, my cabinmates have already left for the mess hall. Which means I'm now officially late.

As I tug off my filthy riding boots and quickly change into sneakers, I notice the corner of a book peeking out from under Nora's single bed. That's odd. I've never seen Nora read in the cabin before. She's usually way too busy prepping for our next day of riding—or slipping into the Land o' Snores the instant her head hits the pillow.

Curious, I slide the book out from beneath the cot. *The Horse Girl's Veterinary Handbook* . . . Wow, who knew the *HGVH* would be the hottest book of the summer??

But wait a second. This looks just like Gwyneth's copy.

I double-check—and yep!—her name is inscribed right on the cover. (As I mentioned a few months ago, horse girls love to put their names on *everything*.)

So why was the *HGVH* under *Nora's* bed?

I reach down to lug the heavy tome back to its proper home. But as I lift the book from the floor, I notice a corner of one of its pages has been carefully folded down. My thumb fiddles with the little creased triangle, and the book (practically!) opens itself.

I skim the dog-eared page as swiftly as I can.

LAMINITIS

Also known as founder, laminitis is an inflammation of the tissue that connects a horse's hoof to the coffin bone in its foot.[1] Ancient fossil evidence suggests that horses have been dealing with laminitis for almost two million years!

Symptoms: A horse with laminitis may have a hoof that is hot to the touch and a faster-than-normal pulse in its fetlock. She may also lean back on her heels, shift her weight while standing, be reluctant to walk, and experience lameness (or limping) while turning.

Treatments: Besides a change of diet and stall rest, laminitis can be treated with special heart-bar horseshoes (shaped like an upside-down heart) fitted by a farrier. The horse can then shift weight from the painful hoof wall to the frog, relieving pressure and helping it heal.[2]

[1] The coffin bone, shaped like a hoof, is at the very bottom of a horse's leg. It connects with the lamina, a type of tissue in the hoof, and helps support the entire weight of your steed. Which could be more than one thousand pounds! In fact, the heaviest horse in history was a shire named Mammoth, who weighed more than three thousand pounds. (That's a lot of NickerDoodles!)

[2] Hiding under a horse's hoof is a "frog"—a fleshy, V-shaped cushion that acts like a shock absorber. It's important to keep it clean and healthy. *(Ribbit-ribbit.)*

That's odd . . . Nora said Balthazar took a hard landing a few months ago but is completely healed. So why would she be reading up on laminitis *now*? Unless . . .

Boom! Before I can do more sleuthing, the heavy book slips from my hands and crashes to the floor. And I'm suddenly startled out of my horse-girl hypnosis.

What am I doing?? I'm already late for dinner, and I can't afford to get into any more trouble. This is *not* the time for equine veterinary research!

As I lean down to grab the *HGVH*, I notice another book—this time a worn paperback—also shoved under Nora's bed. I gingerly drag it out from beneath her cot. When I lift it up, the title practically leaps off the purple cover in bold, black letters . . .

HORSENAPPED!
By Bonnie Bryant[3]

Gasp! I peek inside and find Noel's name scribbled inside. A crescendo of dread rises in my body as I piece together the following two facts:

1. Someone in Misty has been reading about horsenappings.
2. A horse has suddenly gone missing from Misty.

Does this add up to a crime? Or simply excellent taste in

---

[3] *HORSENAPPED!* is the seventeenth book in a popular series called The Saddle Club, written by Bonnie Bryant. It's been a hit with #HorseGirls since the 1980s.

mystery books?? I wish I were better at detective math!

My tummy grumbles loudly, reminding me how late I am for dinner. I shove the books back into place on Gwynnie's and Noey's bunk shelves, then mentally circle Gwyneth, Noel, *and* Nora on my suspect list. I'll have to sort out all these new clues later. Because right now? I *need* to get to the mess hall.

And decide exactly who to tell . . . exactly what I know.

CHAPTER TWENTY

When I burst through the doors of the mess hall, one look at my fellow campers' crestfallen faces leaves me tongue-tied. Instead of a make-believe whodunit, this mystery feels suddenly, frighteningly real.

Gwyneth meets my eyes, then shakes her head sadly. "Mr. Gulch hasn't found Silver Streak," she whispers.

"He and the ranch hands are going back out with flashlights to search again tonight," Everleigh says softly.

"Don't worry, even in my scariest mystery books, everything works out in the end," Noel adds, her voice tinged with worry. "At least . . . most of the time?"

"Mr. Gulch isn't going to give up," Clementine insists.

"*None* of us is giving up," Nora says matter-of-factly, passing an aluminum tray full of something labeled "Mountaintop Skillet Spaghetti" down the table to me.

My tummy grumbles again, and I plop a giant scoop of

the crispy-on-the-outside, ooey-gooey-on-the-inside noodle concoction onto my plate. (Desperate times call for delicious comfort food. *Especially* when said comfort food is a pile of yummy spaghetti wrapped in a hug of fried cheese.)

Amara, however, pushes her plate aside and asks to be excused. She looks even more miserable than before.

Of course she's miserable. We'd all held out hope that Mr. Gulch would bring Silver Streak back home before dark. But they're both still missing. I can't imagine how devastated I'd feel if Clyde Lee or Bandit disappeared . . . and even the grown-ups couldn't find them. My heart aches for Amara.

"I'll wrap up a plate and bring it back to the cabin for you to eat later, Amara," Nora murmurs.

"Silver Streak will turn up, I just know it," Clementine says. "In fact, I had a vision about it! You were both soaking wet and—"

"Amara?" I interrupt, taking a determined breath. "There are some important things I need to tell you—"

But Amara scowls and flips her glossy hair. "In case you weren't paying attention, Willa, I'm not really in the mood for story time??" She shoves her chair away from the table, covers her face in her hands, and rushes out the door before I can tell her what I've learned. (Or, um, ask her about her secret brother.)

A glum silence falls over the dinner table. Noel and Everleigh half-heartedly shovel bites of food into their mouths, but even *I* have lost my appetite. For perhaps the first time in my fourteen-year existence.

Eventually, we all troop back to Misty. Nora carries a foil-wrapped plate of food, but Amara has already cocooned herself beneath her cotton-candy duvet.

"Reckon it's best to let her sleep," Nora says with a sigh.

The Claremont sisters and Clementine nod, then flop onto their beds. Nora suggests we write letters home or make friendship bracelets. But it's hard to concentrate when we're all worried sick for Amara—and Silver Streak.

I'm dying to tell everyone about his missing hay and snacks and saddle. And the books I just discovered under Nora's bed. And how Pasquale is actually Amara's stepbrother(?!). And mostly? How it's NOT MY FAULT that Silver Streak is gone!

But the moment feels all wrong. Nobody seems in the mood to chitchat about clues or family trees or books. So I decide to keep everything to myself for now, at least until I can eliminate my fellow Misty-mates from the suspect list. Or? (Gulp.) The exact opposite . . .

I climb up to my bunk as quietly as I can. But as I reach the top of the ladder and am about to tug the suspect list from my pocket, I notice an envelope lying on my bed.

"Forgot to tell ya, Wills, you got a special delivery while you were mucking out stalls," Nora says with a wink.

I flip over the letter. It's postmarked Nebraska. And addressed to "Ms. Willa Watkins, Horse Girl Extraordinaire."

CHAPTER TWENTY-ONE

Dear Willa,

Happy First Week of Horse Camp!! Your mom and I (and yes, Kay, too 😊) sure hope you're having one heck of a galloping summer.

(I can see you rolling your eyes about my #HorseDad jokes from here.)

The Juniper Ranch Parents Handbook suggested we snail-mail you a letter <u>before</u> camp starts so it'll arrive during your first week. I'm hoping you wrote us a letter, too, just like you promised. (Hint, hint!) But I suppose we won't know for a while because, according to the old handbook, letters can take

<u>weeks</u> to arrive. (Where's the Pony Express when you need it??)

The Juniper Ranch folks say it's important for you to have a chance to "establish your independence" without phone calls or emails from home, so your mom and I are going to try to be patient... even if we sure as heck don't like it!

I'm writing this before we drove to Colorado, but there's a 95 percent chance I need to apologize for getting a little emotional in front of your horse friends when we said goodbye at camp drop-off. (And by "horse friends," I mean people who are your friends who like horses, as well as horses who are your friends who like people. You get it!) Anyhoo, I'm going to go ahead and assume I started bawling my eyes out. It's just so hard to believe <u>both</u> my girls are going to be gone all summer. In fact, all <u>three</u> of my ladies are gone if you count Mom. Which I definitely do. (Dang it, please ignore the teardrops on this letter.)

BUT. I am <u>so</u> proud of you for chasing your Horse Girl dreams. And your mom is just bursting her buttons for you. She wanted to write you a letter from her base, but we figured it wouldn't reach you until <u>next</u> summer, so she and I are writing this letter together during our FaceTime date night.

(I can hear you saying ewwww from here.)

Speaking of, your mom and I have some big news for you when you get back! Your mom made me promise to keep it secret for now, but as soon as you and Kay are both home, we'll fill you in.

In the meantime, we hope you're having a gosh-darn ball with all your friends from Oakwood. Hope you're making lots of new friends, too, kiddo! We can't wait to hear about all the horses you're getting to ride and all the new equestrian skills you're learning and, most of all, all the memories you're making. This is what it's all about, Wills.

And if you happen to be a teeny-tiny bit homesick (which I'm sure you're not), just remember to look up to those stars at night and know your family is looking at the same stars—no matter how far apart we are, your mom and I will find the Pegasus constellation in the sky and think of our girls. (The winged horse shape reminds us of you, the "orange supergiant star of spectral type K21b" reminds us of Kay.) Oh gosh, now I'm crying again.

   I know Clyde Lee will be excited to hear all about horse camp as soon as you're back. And so will the rest of us. Keep riding high, kiddo!

   We love ya lots,
   Dad (+ Mom + Kay + Clyde Lee)

CHAPTER TWENTY-TWO

Big news??

I flip the letter over and read it again, desperate to find a hint that I've missed somewhere in my dad's words.

"Big news" might mean a lot of different things in lots of other families. But in a military family like mine, it means only one thing. The worst thing.

We're moving. Again.

THIS. CANNOT. BE. HAPPENING.

Just when I *finally* found my forever friends at Oakwood (well, except for maybe Amara) and *finally* became a real rider (kind of) and *finally* got to go to horse camp (unless I get kicked out tomorrow), my parents are now going to make me move. And take all of that away from me. For the gazillionth time. What if we end up in another country again? Like Germany? Or Liechtenstein! Do they even have horses in Liechtenstein??

Then another possibility occurs to me. An even worse possibility. What if my mom's deployment is being extended? And she has to stay on the other side of the world for another year without us? Have I mentioned THIS CANNOT BE HAPPENING???

Mom *promised* me she'd be coming home at the end of the summer. She *swore*. She said if we could just be strong and make it through this really tough year, we'd all be together again, and everything would be back to normal.

I know her career is super important, but aren't we important, too?? I'm sick of looking up in the sky for Pegasus. I want to look up and see my mom. Right next to me.

I know that my dad would say I'm jumping to conclusions right now without any evidence. And my mom would say not to throw the baby out with the bathwater. (Her metaphors are almost as dramatic and confusing as I am!)

But this "good news" thing *cannot* be good. My dad was trying to sound super cheerful in his letter, but it's obvious he was just pretending everything's fine so that I don't get upset and ruin horse camp.

Well, news flash, Dad . . . I've *already* ruined horse camp!!

I decide I'm not going to sit around and wait for my parents to pick me up and tell me the "big news." Or wait for Mr. Gulch to blame me for Amara's horse going missing and kick me out. This whole thing has been a massive mistake. There's only one thing left for me to do . . .

I'm going to call my parents and tell them I'm quitting horse camp.

"Everything okay, Wills?"

Startled, I look up to see Gwyneth staring at me—and at the letter furiously balled up in my hand. Guess I was grunting to conclusions a little loudly.

"I'm fine," I say, but my voice quavers as I shove the crinkled letter under my pillow.

"Listen, mates," Nora announces. "We've all had a rough day. I say we call it an early night and start fresh tomorrow."

Ugh, the last thing I want to think about right now is fresh starts in my life. Dad's letter feels like a ticking time bomb beneath my pillow.

"We have a big day ahead of us," Nora says brightly, rising from her cot and striding across the cabin toward the light switch. "Tomorrow is Horseback Swim!"

And suddenly, grins bound across the faces of all the Misty campers. Despite the tsunami of emotions brewing inside my body and my growing mountain of worries, even *I* can't help lighting up as I imagine the enchanted ride through the waters of Juniper Creek.

In fact, the only one *not* smiling right now is Amara. At least I *assume* she's not smiling? She's still bunkered beneath her blankets and refuses to emerge, let alone emote.

"I know it's been a dodgy couple of days," Nora continues. "But I want you to remember why we're here. It's because we all—every last one of us—love horses more than anything in the world. I don't want you to miss out on the magic of your summer at Camp Juniper. So tomorrow we're going to forget our worries, if only for a few hours . . . and take our gentle giants for a dip!"

At the end of her speech, Nora dramatically flips off the lights like a magician pulling a disappearing act.

And I silently wonder if I can maybe wait . . . just one more *teeny-tiny* day . . . before I quit horse camp.

CHAPTER TWENTY-THREE

Clang-clang . . . Clang-clang . . . Clang-clang.

I shoot awake, bolting upright in my bunk (*owwww!*) as Big Ben peals away. I glance around at my Misty cabinmates. I know we're all hoping against hope that the clanging means Silver Streak has been found.

But as I wipe the sleep from my eyes, I realize it's just the regular morning bell, waking us for (as Nora calls it) "brekkie."

After we troop to the mess hall and slurp our cereal, Griff—the boys' counselor from King of the Wind—comes over to whisper in Nora's ear. (Which, of course, we can all hear, because grown-ups always *think* they're quieter talkers than they really are.)

Nora's ear-to-ear grin quickly deflates, as Griff reports that Mr. Gulch is still out searching, deeper into neighboring ranches far beyond Camp Juniper. He's instructed the counselors to pretend everything's normal so as not to cause a panic. But Silver Streak is still missing. And (at least as far as anyone else knows) . . . it's still my fault.

While the other tables are filled with carefree campers singing songs at the top of their lungs, trading friendship bracelets, and playing the cup game with wild abandon, a cloud of gloom falls over the Misty breakfast table.

Nora tears her gaze away from Griff and attempts to chase our sadness away.

"No worries, mates! Mr. Gulch must have found an important clue, or he would have come back last night. Silver Streak probably just wandered over to another ranch, where he could find food and water. He's a clever boy! And Mr. Gulch will have a far better chance of finding him in the daylight."

I glance around the table. Nobody looks particularly convinced by Nora's pep talk. Amara barely seems to be listening. Instead, she's wriggling around on the bench, furiously scratching her arms.

"Up and at 'em! We've got a date with a creek," Nora cajoles. "Your horses are probably already wearing their water wings!"

We slowly rise from the wooden table and carry our trays to the kitchen. But Amara stays put, still clawing at her arms.

"I'm not going."

"Aw, Amara," Nora answers. "I know you're upset, but staying behind won't—"

"Poison ivy!" Amara wails miserably. "I'm covered with it! And it's all that stupid pony's fault. Lasagna kept dragging me through the branches and vines and who knows what else on our trail ride yesterday."

"I think the pony's preferred name is Macaroni?" Clementine offers gently.

Amara's eyes flash with anger. "Macaroni? Lasagna?? What's the difference?? Olive Garden the Horse gave me a rash!"

"Blimey," Nora whispers as she examines Amara's forearm, which is smothered in pink dots. "We better get you to the infirmary."

"Fine," Amara sniffs. "But I'll be sending Linguine the bill for my dermatologist once I get home."

Nora raises an eyebrow, then ushes Amara out of the mess hall and down the trail toward the nurse's cabin.

By the time Nora returns and meets the rest of us in the paddock, the sun is high in the sky, beating down on us.

"Gonna be a scorcher!" Nora grins. "Can't think of better weather for a swim."

"Will Amara be okay?" I ask, worry throttling my voice.

(The voice in my head asks the same question about Silver Streak.)

"A little calamine lotion and a day of pampering from the nurse, and she'll be right as rain," Nora reassures me with a wink. "And I have a strong feeling Mr. Gulch is going to bring Silver Streak home safe and sound by the time we're back, so don't fret about that either."

Nora has an uncanny knack for cheering me up (and reading my mind). *Unless* . . . she's only covering her tracks??

"Now, everybody grab a helmet and a life jacket. Let's saddle up!"

A flicker of joy flutters in my chest as I snap on the bright orange inflatable vest along with my helmet.

Bandit, handsome as always, nickers as I approach his stall. But when he sees my Day-Glo life jacket, he lets out a loud snort.

"Easy boy," I giggle, letting him sniff my life preserver and giving him a gentle pat to keep him calm.

I briefly consider dragging everyone over to Silver Streak's stall to show them the clues I found yesterday. But I stop myself. Because as important as the missing saddle and hay and NickerDoodles are (not to mention the mysterious text message and books and stepbrother!), they don't actually explain what—or *who*—caused Silver Streak to go missing. They only prove that *someone* took him.

Which I'm not sure I should keep reminding everyone

at the moment . . . especially when Nora's trying so hard to cheer us all up.

And besides, this may be my very last day at horse camp. If Mr. Gulch comes back empty-handed tonight, I'm 99 percent certain I'll be sent home. Amara will make sure of that. So I may as well enjoy my last few glorious hours at Juniper Ranch.

Unless . . .

It's still *possible* that Mr. Gulch will find Silver Streak, right? And this big mystery will turn out to be just a giant misunderstanding? And I'll get to stay at horse camp forever and never deal with the "big news" from home??

(Ugh, the stupid hope in my stupid horse-girl heart just keeps bubbling to the top, no matter how many times I try to shove it back down.)

Nora, Clem, the Claremont triplets, and I mount up and set off down Juniper Creek Run at a quick trot. A thrill of anticipation floats in the air. We lean forward in our saddles—each searching for the first glimmer of water.

Even the horses are excited. It's hard to keep Bandit from zipping into a canter and crashing ahead of the line. He knows there's an equine splash zone waiting for him at the bottom of the trail's switchbacks!

And suddenly, we see it: the shimmering waters of Juniper

Creek. All of us—the girls *and* the horses—are champing at the bit to dive in.[1]

But Nora stops us with a loud "whoa," then instructs us to dismount.

"We can't afford to lose another saddle to the bottom of the creek. Let's take 'em off."

After tying our horses' leads to a hitching post near the water's edge, we uncinch their saddle girths and heave the heavy leather seats and sweaty saddle pads onto a log that's been fashioned into a long saddle bench. Both the hitching post and the bench seem to have been carved just for this occasion—the horse version of a swimming pool locker room.

"Horses are born swimmers," Nora explains as she walks down the line of campers, double-checking our helmets and life jackets for snugness. "Mind you, some of them are more enthusiastic about it than others . . ."

She nods toward Bandit, who's lurching on his lead, gazing longingly at the water.

He lets out a loud *pfffffff* and paws the ground impatiently.

"Soon, boy," I laugh, pushing him back a bit to square him up with the other horses, all patiently waiting their turn

---

[1] Inspired by restless horses chewing and grinding on their bits while waiting to move, the phrase "champing at the bit" refers to anyone who's eager or impatient to get to something. Like when I'm champing at the bit for more chockie!

while we riders slip off our boots and socks.

"I'm glad you all passed your swim tests, but we're going to let the horses take the lead today," Nora instructs us. "Keep a loose rein and give them plenty of room to move their heads naturally above the water, so they feel like they're in control. Remember: They're Esther Williams, and you're just the swim cap!"[2]

We all laugh, and I know *exactly* what to put on my next #HorseGirl T-shirt.

Next Nora teaches us how to mount our horses—bareback! "Once you've learned this skill, you can combine it with the running mount we worked on yesterday with Macaroni. In case you ever have an emergency on the trail."

She steps closer to Balthazar to demonstrate.

"Just like with the running mount, you want to face your horse's rump with your left hand on his neck, grab a handful of mane near the withers, push off hard from your left leg, then swing your right leg over your horse's back, swiveling your hips. Try to bring your seat down gently in the saddle area. And don't worry, I'll give you a leg up if you need a boost!"

One by one, Nora helps us swing ourselves aboard. Everleigh, of course, is a natural—leaping onto Sierra like

---

2   Esther Williams was a famous swimmer and film actress who starred in many "aquamusicals," which featured synchronized swimming and diving. While horses have to keep their heads above water, they still know how to make a splash, just like Esther!

she's Simone Biles nailing a double layout. Noel carefully tucks her glasses into her breeches pocket before hopping aboard Tango. ("If they fall off in the water, they could slice someone!" she explains ominously.) Gwyneth pinpoints the exact anatomical location of Romeo's withers before she attempts her mount. Clementine, meanwhile, pinpoints the exact location of Aurora's *aura*.

When it's finally my turn, I can't help giggling with glee as I gently land atop Bandit. It's absolutely electrifying to feel his strength beneath me, my long legs dangling down his barrel—no saddle or stirrups between us. "It's just you and me, boy!" I whisper.

"Stretch out your legs and sink back into your balance point," Nora instructs us once we're mounted up. "Keep your body relaxed and your heels down.[3] We're going to walk *very* slowly."

She leads our slow-motion stroll to the water. I ever-so-gently squeeze Bandit's sides, and we fall in line with the other horses stepping gingerly down the slanted bank. It's finally time for splashdown!

Bandit's hooves *clop-clop* over the smooth, round stones at the edge of the creek. I keep his reins long and let him

---

[3] "Heels down!" is something you hear yelled a lot during riding lessons. You're supposed to let your weight fall down into your heels, instead of your toes. It keeps your legs relaxed, your center of gravity low, and your head-shoulders-hips-heels in a straight line. (Sing it with me: "Head, shoulders, hips, and heels, hips and heels!")

guide us into the burbling, crystal-clear water.[4] "I can see the bottom!" I whisper with wonder.

Without further ado, Bandit storms in—and I feel myself going in, too! First my toes, then my ankles, then—*whoosh!*—I'm belly deep and half floating!

"This is the best feeling in the world!" I squeal.

"It's c-c-c-c-c-cold!" Everleigh yelps through chattering teeth, as she and Sierra wade in beside us.

"The ice melt from the top of the mountain is reffffffffreshing!" Gwyneth shivers as Romeo marches in deeper. Now he's entirely submerged in the water—with only his ears, eyes, and nose peeking out!

"Juniper Creek may be chilly, but it's known for its healing powers," Clementine explains, reaching down to gently pat Aurora's neck. "For our bodies and our spirits!"

"And our horsesssss!" Noel giggles-slash-shivers.

She keeps her steed, Tango, safely in the shallow edge of the stream. But he's having a ball, stomping his front hooves as hard as he can to splash the water. And, naturally, anyone nearby.

"Good boy," she praises him, wiping her now-soaking-wet hair out of her eyes as he makes mountainous splashes in the baby-pool section of the creek.

Bandit, however, ventures farther into the deeper, big-kid

---

4   Also known as "free rein" or "giving your horse his head," keeping the reins long allows horses to move freely and feel in charge. Because, just like us, horses want to be their own boss sometimes, too!

waters. He's now actually swimming—I can feel his hooves dog-paddling (make that *horse*-paddling!) weightlessly. The water's now *above* my belly button.

"You guys, we're *swimming*!" I squeal.

"On our horses!" Gwyneth adds giddily.

"I reckoned you'd like it," Nora laughs as she and Balthazar swim laps around us.

"It's like *Misty of Chincoteague* IRL," Gwyneth sighs.

I imagine I'm floating with the ponies across the channel from Assateague to Chincoteague Island, just like in Marguerite Henry's famous book. "Not only are we living in Misty, but now we're swimming like her, too!"[5]

This has got to be one of the most epic, top-ten moments in my life. Or the life of any horse girl. *Blimey*, I wish I could stay at horse camp forever . . .

I glance down at my GRIT bracelet, now flecked with water. It reminds me that I still have a choice.

I can run away from camp, giving up on all my #HorseGirl dreams—and friends—just because I'm afraid they'll be taken away from me. Or I can fight like heck to keep them. And use everything I've learned along the way to *prove* that I belong here.

Which means saving Silver Streak . . . before it's too late.

---

[5] Marguerite Henry's beloved novel *Misty of Chincoteague* was inspired by the real-life Pony Swim each summer between Assateague and Chincoteague Islands in Virginia (and a real-life palomino pinto named Misty).

CHAPTER TWENTY-FOUR

Screeeeeeech.

I push open the screen door to the Craft Shack the next morning. It's camper free hour, so we can choose any activity we like—swimming, hiking, bird-watching or (drumroll, please) horseback riding. It's a cornucopia of choices!

But what horse girl on the planet would choose lanyard making over jumping a magnificent steed? *This* crazy horse girl. Because . . . *dun, dun, duuuuun* . . . it means I'll have the Craft Shack all to myself!

I told Nora that I wanted to get a jump start on Bandit's costume for Camp Games. (Apparently all the Juniper Ranch campers disguise their horses as different animals on the last day of camp, and we play mounted games like tag or Red Light, Green Light, while riding "lions" and "tigers" and "unicorns," oh my!)

But here's my *real* plan: I'll grab some Pony Paint and

ribbons from the Craft Shack so it looks like I was busy making Bandit's costume. Then I'll quickly sneak back to Misty before the other girls return, to do more sleuthing in the cabin without anyone noticing.

(Am I a brilliant horse detective or what?)

I can't stop thinking about the books I found in the cabin yesterday—and whether someone in Misty was actually studying how to be a horse thief. And/or an equine infectious disease specialist.

I need to figure out how those clues connect with the missing saddle and hay and NickerDoodles. I must have missed something important that could help me figure out exactly who took Silver Streak. And *why*. And *where* on earth they might be hiding him . . .

Because Mr. Gulch still isn't back. He radioed the counselors last night to report there may be another wild mustang herd roaming in the area. He said he wants to search a few more ranches before he returns to Juniper.

Which means? I've got to activate GRIT mode!

I swiftly scan the art-supply shelf in the Craft Shack to snag what I need and be on my way. The Pony Paint is carefully organized in a rainbow of hues.[1] But there's an empty circle on the dusty shelf . . . exactly where the pink paint bottles should be.

---

[1] Pony Paint is a kind of liquid chalk paint that's totally safe for horses. It washes out with a little shampoo and a good brushing. I learned about it last fall during the Oakwood Riding Academy's annual Halloween parade!

"That's weird," I mumble.

"My shirt?" a low voice asks. "I thought it was hilarious, but . . . too far?"

I whirl around, startled. My eyes flick up to see an emerald green pair smiling back at me. I gaze into them for a moment—*mesmerized*—until I remember that Pasquale just mentioned his T-shirt. And that I should probably, you know, look at it. Instead of staring at his eyeballs.

I force my glance down to the tee, which proclaims in large letters:

WILL TRADE SISTER FOR HORSE

I can't help snorting before I wrangle my smile into a stern frown.

"Pasquale," I scold. "Amara is going through a really hard time—besides her missing horse, she's still in the infirmary."

He lets out a low laugh. "Oh, believe me, I would only dare to wear this when I know she's under medical supervision!"

I giggle guiltily.

"But she actually gave it to me for my birthday last month, so I'm safe." He winks.

"Speaking of your sister, I've, um, been meaning to ask you about the night—"

"What's yours say?" he asks at the exact same time.

I glance down at my own shirt. It's emblazoned with the image of a rider barely clinging on to a rearing horse holding a microphone in its hoof. Below the drawing are the words:

"Ha, that's brilliant! Will you make me one?"

(OMG, Pasquale just asked me to design him a T-shirt! Does this qualify as a fashion emergency??) I'm so euphoric that instead of finishing my question or answering his, I grin at him like a deranged rodeo clown.

"I mean, it's cool if you don't have time."

"The pink Pony Paint is missing!" I blurt, shaking myself out of my haze. I remind myself that I'm *supposed* to be hunting for clues to save Silver Streak, not discussing horse puns with Pasquale.

He blinks several times, then tilts his head in confusion.

"I could, uh, make you some?" he offers. "I don't know if you've heard, but mixing red and white makes . . . wait for it . . . pink."

"Ha—that's brilliant! I mean, I'm not saying you're brilliant just because you just said my T-shirt was brilliant. I'm saying it as a joke. But, like, not that you're *not* smart! Because you are! I mean, not that I've noticed because I'm obsessed with—"

OMG, someone stop me.

"Anyway! Yes! I'll mix up the paint, great idea! But, um? Right now? I should probably get going."

I start to dash out of the room, but Pasquale calls after me.

"Hey, don't I get a NickerDoodle for saving the day?" He pantomimes pulling one of the treats out of his pocket, tossing it in the air, and gobbling it down like a Scooby Snack.

I didn't think it was possible, but the clown grin on my face grows even larger. As does the splotch of red that's now covering my cheeks. *(Do they make a cream to stop uncontrollable blushing? Cuz that's one lotion I would actually buy.)*

"Okay, then, bye now!" I yelp, snatching a feathery pink boa from the supply shelf as I push past him and rush out the door.

Pasquale gives me a small, bewildered wave goodbye.

As I slip down the secret trail back to Misty, something nags at me (besides the missing pink Pony Paint and my mortifying dissertation on whether or not Pasquale is, in fact, brilliant).

The NickerDoodles . . .

Pasquale was the one who told me about the NickerDoodles in the first place. And he's the one who brought them to the stable. Then, later, the box of fancy snacks went missing. And so did Silver Streak . . .

CHAPTER TWENTY-FIVE

I crouch behind Misty, listening carefully for the signs of any stragglers who might have stayed in their bunks for free hour. But the only sound I hear is the wind rushing through the nearby quaking aspen trees.

I slink around to the front of the cabin, climb up the worn wooden steps, and slip through the screen door. (Still no screech—Amara's face cream really is a miracle worker!)

I'm hoping the two books I found last night will have more clues about what happened to Silver Streak. I decide to start with Gwyneth's bookshelf and the *HGVH*.

But as I lean down into her bottom bunk, something catches my eye in the corner of the room, near Amara's bed.

I walk over to investigate—then stop dead in my tracks.

Lying on top of the sea of pink in Amara's bunk is a note. Its letters have been cut and pasted from a magazine, and a small lock of braided black hair dangles next to it.

We have the creature
that you seek,
your beloved steed,
Silver Streak.
Don't tell the adults
this note has arrived,
if you hope to see your
horse alive.
To save his tail and
beautiful coat,
get $1 million and wait
for a note.

CHAPTER TWENTY-SIX

I nearly scream, but clamp a hand over my mouth, dropping the letter to the floor in the process. The horse-tail braid helicopters to the ground next to the note, its black strands as familiar to me as if they were my own hair.

"Silver Streak!" I whisper in horror. I'm suddenly dizzy... and feel like I might be sick.

All this time I've secretly hoped I was wrong, and that Nora and Mr. Gulch were right. That Silver Streak somehow just wandered off into a neighboring ranch (maybe he put his saddle on himself?) or was "borrowed" by a vet or handler who confused him (and his famous white star?) with another horse. As much fun as I was having sleuthing, deep down I believed everything would solve itself—like an episode of a silly TV show where it's all a big misunderstanding and then everyone laughs in the end.

But it's obvious now that there's not going to be any

laughing. This is no innocent mix-up or imaginary crime. Silver Streak has been horsenapped. *For real.*

I start to cry out for help, but the note's magazine-cutout letters glare up at me with their ominous warning:

> **DON'T TELL THE ADULTS THIS NOTE HAS ARRIVED, IF YOU HOPE TO SEE YOUR HORSE ALIVE.**

Ugh, blergh, blimey, crikey!!!! Despite all my Nancy Drewing around camp looking for clues, the truth is, I have no idea how to solve a real-life, actual, super-scary mystery. I glance back down at the note.

> **TO SAVE HIS TAIL AND BEAUTIFUL COAT, GET $1 MILLION AND WAIT FOR A NOTE.**

And then it hits me. There's only one person who could help me save Silver Streak right now . . .

Amara.

(Or more precisely? Her mom's bank account.)

Chapter Twenty-Seven

I bound down the camp path and hurl myself toward the infirmary, dashing as quietly as I can up the steps of the front porch. I crouch low and lean my ear against the door. I somehow have to get inside without alerting any adults. The ransom note made that terrifyingly clear.

My heart hammers in my chest as I listen closely at the door. Thankfully, what I hear may be my new favorite sound on earth.

Zzzzzzzzzz. Zzzzzzzzz.

I oh-so-gently push the door open to find Mrs. Hailey, Camp Juniper's nurse, fast asleep in her chair, her curly white hair exploding in all directions from the top of her blue scrubs. A thin line of drool dangles from her lips down to the stethoscope draped around her neck.

Phew.

"Amara?" I whisper, glancing around the cots lining the pine walls of the cabin. Green curtained dividers offer a small dose of privacy between the cots, but it seems the infirmary is empty, except for the snoozing Mrs. Hailey and one bed—where a single sick camper is tucked completely beneath the blankets.

"*Amara?!*" I whisper again, tiptoeing over to her cot. "We need to talk."

But Amara stays silent. She's clearly still furious with me. Even though I now have evidence that *proves* I'm not the reason Silver Streak is missing.

Still, I dread having to tell her about the ransom note—the truth may be better for me, but it's horrifying for poor Silver Streak.

"Amara, I know you're super mad at me, but this is super important! I found a note in your bunk and—"

Ka-ka-ka-koooooooooooo!!

The honk of Mrs. Hailey's snore startles me. I practically jump in the air, then fall forward onto Amara's cot. *Eeeeeep!*

But instead of crashing into her body, I land on something soft and smooshy. Confused, I fling away the comforter to reveal . . . a pile of pillows. Which are covered with pink polka dots. (*Of course* they are. Because Amara is the only person on the planet who'd bring her own custom pink pillows along to the infirmary!)

But as far Amara herself? She's nowhere to be found.

OMG.

OMG.

OMG.

The horsenappers must have taken her, too!

CHAPTER TWENTY-EIGHT

I spin on my heels and dash out the infirmary door, praying the screen-door slam doesn't wake the snoring Mrs. Hailey. (News flash: It does not!) Then I fly down the main camp trail back to the cabin.

My only hope in the world is that while I was heading to the infirmary, Amara took the secret path back to Misty and we just missed each other, like stallions passing in the night.

But as I run inside, the cabin is still empty. Amara is still missing. And this is still *not* good.

My hands start to shake as I try to catch my breath. *This is all my fault.* I was so certain that if I solved the mystery by myself, I'd prove to everyone (especially myself) that I truly belong here. But if I'd just told someone, *anyone* about the clues I found in the barn two days ago, then maybe Mr. Gulch would have found Silver Streak by now, and Amara would be safe and sound and scratching away in the infirmary.

How could I have been so selfish?!

Even worse? I'm now completely alone.

I glance up to my top bunk and the photos I taped up on my first day of camp. I stare at the one of me and my family. I never thought I'd say this, but I'd give anything to have my parents here right now, telling me exactly what to do. Heck, I'd even take Kay calling it "farm camp" and sneezing orders at me.

Then I look over to the pic of me, Amara, Gwyneth, Everleigh, and Noel (and our horses, of course) at the Oakwood Invitational a few months ago.

I never could have survived last year if it weren't for my forever herd. I'm suddenly flooded with memories . . . like how scary it was to jump (and fall on my face!) for the first time . . . and how hard it was for me to trust them at first . . . how I finally let them into my heart . . . and how they cheered me on with their amazing secret notes.

And then it hits me. Maybe I'm not alone, after all. The ransom note said not to tell any *adults*. But it didn't say anything about friends . . .

I quickly tear off a page of paper from my notebook and scribble a message for Gwen, Everleigh, and Noel, which I tuck inside the open *HGVH* on Gwyn's bed.

CHAPTER TWENTY-NINE

Thump-thump, thump-thump.

My heart thunders as I crouch in Silver Streak's stall, waiting for Gwyn, Ev, and Noey. The stall is as empty as it was the last time I was here. The hay and NickerDoodles and saddle are still missing. And so, of course, are Silver Streak and Amara.

But I can't just sit around doing nothing while I wait for the Oakwood Flyers to arrive. I quickly yank the suspect list from my breeches pocket.

I immediately circle SCARY HORSE THIEVES in a thick line with my pencil.

BUT . . . could someone *else* on the suspect list have helped them? I scan through the remaining names, one by one.

The Claremont triplets: The *HORSENAPPED!* novel definitely belongs to Noel, which clearly links her to the crime. But *The Horse Girl's Veterinary Handbook* belongs to Gwyneth, which links *her* to the crime! But I found both of them under *Nora's* bed, which clearly links *her* to the crime! The truth is, anyone in Misty could have taken the books when Gwyn and Noey weren't paying attention, then shoved them under Nora's bed to hide them.

Then there's Everleigh. She brought a bunch of *Young Rider* and *Inside Gymnastics* magazines to camp. And the letters on the ransom note were torn out of (drumroll, please!) magazines. Could Ev have quietly pasted the note together while the rest of us were sleeping? She would have had to borrow scissors and glue from the Craft Shack. So maybe she also had a little help from her triplets-in-crime, Gwyneth and Noel??

The Claremont sisters are definitely smart enough to plan a real-life horse mystery. But they've been friends with Amara for forever—why would they ever want to hurt her . . . or Silver Streak??

Clementine: Clem is the only girl in our cabin who's *not* an Oakwood Flyer. But maybe she followed Amara on

HorseTube and knew exactly how valuable her horse was? Whoa, whoa, whoa . . . maybe Clem's not even a real camper! Maybe she's a spy who works for professional horse thieves who sign her up for equestrian camps across the country to find perfect ponies for the bad guys to steal?!? At this point, I cannot rule anything out!

Nora: As sweet as she seems, Nora told us that she had to wait for Balthazar to be "100 percent" before she could go back to her dream job as a stunt rider in Hollywood. Maybe Nora borrowed Gwyneth's vet book to read more about his injury? Maybe, *maybe*, she learned something she didn't like . . . so she decided to steal Amara's horse to replace Balthazar? Which would explain why she *also* had Noel's *HORSENAPPED!* book in her possession??

Mr. Gulch: When I think back, I realize that Mr. Gulch was the very last person in the barn with Silver Streak after Pasquale and I snuck away through the paddock. The hay and NickerDoodles and saddle were still there before we left . . . then they were gone the next morning, along with Silver Streak. And Gulch has been out searching for a *long* time. What if he's not actually searching? What if he's . . . *horsenapping*??

It makes complete sense! Mr. Gulch keeps dropping hints that Camp Juniper is struggling to stay afloat and that he might have to shut it down next year. Silver Streak is a super valuable horse. Gwyneth said he's worth more than a house! Or—perhaps—more than a horse camp?!

Mr. Gulch must know plenty of ranchers and show jumpers who'd just love to buy a horse like that. And Mr. Gulch was the one who insisted nobody in our cabin tell their parents about Silver Streak going missing.

Maybe Amara somehow figured out his plan—and Mr. Gulch had to kidnap *her* as well to stop her from telling her parents??

Pasquale: Eeek, why are my armpits sweating? *Blergh! Stop it, armpits, I need all my sweat to focus!* Ahem. I know I've been distracted by Pasquale and his clever shirts and eyeballs, but *he* was the one who brought the NickerDoodles to Silver Streak the day I met him at the barn. Just hours before the NickerDoodles—*and Silver Streak*—went missing.

Then something else flashes in my mind. Pasquale was acting strangely when I ran into him in the Craft Shack. He was blinking *a lot*. At first I thought it was just because I was acting so weird. But let's face it—I am *always* acting so weird. So what if he was actually blinking out of nervousness?

Because I happened to walk in just after he'd CRAFTED A RANSOM NOTE FOR HIS NEW SISTER'S HORSE??

GASP!

Pasquale and Amara clearly have some kind of major stepsibling awkwardness going on . . . Could he have been trying to sabotage her jumping career in order to break up Amara's dad's marriage to his mom? Or maybe . . . he just wanted the million-dollar ransom to buy his own new horse??

GASP again!!

The Ghost of Marley: Ghorsts can't hold scissors to make ransom notes. That's just common knowledge. Marley is officially in the clear.

With a great flourish, I cross his name off the suspect list. So that only leaves . . .

Almost everyone else. *Blergh.* Updating this list was clearly a waste of time.

And time is the one thing Silver Streak and Amara don't have right now. I don't even know if Gwyneth will find my emergency-meeting note in the *HGVH*! And if I'm not back at the cabin soon, Nora—*an adult*—will come looking for me and probably find the ransom note in my pocket and then *who knows* what the horsenappers will do??

I drop my head in my hands in frustration and crumple to the ground of the stall.

But, as I blink sideways on the floor, something catches my eye just outside of Silver Streak's stall. I drag myself closer to the shape in the dirt of the barn aisle. It's a heart.

Oh. 😌

The same heart I found etched in the dirt last time I was here with Pasquale. Back when horse camp was still wonderful and magical and . . .

Suddenly, an image of another heart flashes in my mind . . .

The heart-bar horseshoe. From the laminitis page flipped open in *The Horse Girl's Veterinary Handbook*. What if the heart in the dirt wasn't a drawing from Pasquale? What if it was . . .

A hoofprint?!?!

CHAPTER THIRTY

"Wills??" a voice hisses outside the stall door.

"In here!" I hiss back, carefully unlatching Silver Streak's stall door. I watch three identical blond heads—and one purple—bob inside.

"What's *she* doing here?" I whisper, nodding to the purple noggin. "I called for a meeting of the Oakwood Flyers. Clementine is definitely *not* an Oakwood Flyer. I haven't even crossed her off my suspect list! She could be a secret agent for a horsenapping ring!"

They all look at me like I've grown a tail.

"What are you talking about, Wills??" Everleigh asks.

"Your note really scared us." Noel frowns.

"Are you feeling okay?" Gwyneth pulls me aside, her face clouding with concern.

"No! I mean, yes! I mean . . . I . . ."

My brain tries to compute which of the five million

important things I should tell them first. I eventually decide on all of them, whirling out a tornado of words.

"Silver Streak! And Amara! And the saddle's gone! And also? NickerDoodles! And books? And *magazines*! Clem's got a double life! Pasquale in the Craft Shack! With the Pony Paint! Plus hearts! In the stall!"

"Whoa, whoa, whoa, slow down, Wills," Gwyneth says.

"How about some deep breaths?" Clementine demonstrates a long, peaceful exhale from her belly.

I shake my head and fling the ransom note out of my pocket—holding it up in the air as I'm still half hyperventilating. After a quick breath, I finally spit it out.

"Silver Streak's been horsenapped! And Amara's gone missing! And we have to save them both!!"

Their jaws all drop.

I hurriedly fill them in on the entire saga: all the clues I found in the stall and in the cabin, along with the ransom note on Amara's bunk (with the shocking lock of Silver Streak's hair) and the fact that Amara was missing when I went to check on her in the infirmary.

"Why didn't you tell us all of this before?!" Everleigh cries.

"Don't you trust us?" Noel's lip is trembling.

"Of course I trust you!" I insist. "I mean, except for the fact that you're all still on my suspect list."

The girls exchange confused glances.

"I'll explain later. But it's *me* that I didn't trust. After Amara blamed me for leaving the paddock gate open, I assumed you all blamed me as well. And that maybe you wouldn't believe me about the clues I'd found, that you'd think I was just making it up so I wouldn't get in trouble. It was stupid of me, I know, but . . . I was scared I'd lose the only real friends I've ever had."

There's a pause.

Then Gwyneth gives me a wink. "You've got to do a lot worse than that to lose us, Wills."

"Yeah, we're your forever herd!" Everleigh flings her arms into a gymnastics salute.

"Which means, like . . . forever!" Noel adds, before stealthily glancing from side to side. "Unless the kidnappers get us first."

"For the record, I solemnly swear that I am not a secret spy for a horsenapping ring." Clementine raises her hand in the air like she's taking an oath. "But I get it if you need to spy on me to be sure. I'm the new kid, after all . . . and a Gemini riding a Scorpio horse! It makes total sense I could have a double life!"

I LOL. Literally.

"You used to be the new kid, too," Gwyneth reminds me. "When you first came to Oakwood, we weren't sure if we could trust you either. But we gave you a chance."

"So did Amara," Everleigh says, grasping the top edge of the stall and hoisting herself into a pull-up. "At least in her own way?"

"It's just like riding a new horse," Gwyneth continues.

"You use your best instincts, you protect yourself . . . but sometimes you've got to take a leap of faith if you really want to soar together."

"Or fall on your rumps together!" Everleigh adds with a giggle, dropping back down to the ground.

"I'm really sorry, Clementine. I shouldn't have suspected you of anything just because I didn't know you," I say remorsefully. "But if it makes you feel better? I also suspected everyone else in our cabin, so you're in great company."

"That strangely *does* make me feel better." She grins.

I throw one of my extra-long arms around her shoulder. "Welcome to our forever herd!"

"Um, guys? Not to interrupt," Noel interrupts. "But could we save the group hug for when there's not a kid-slash-horsenapper on the loose?"

"Good point," I nod.

"We have a few hours to sneak out while Nora is busy with the all-counselor meeting in the mess hall," Clementine says. "They're in a tizzy trying to run the place without Mr. Gulch."

"Wills, do you have an idea who the horsenappers might be?" Everleigh asks.

"Or where they could have taken Silver Streak and Amara?" Gwyneth adds.

I shake my head, devastated that I have nothing to show for all my sleuthing.

But then a shape flashes in my mind. The clue I found

just before my Misty-mates arrived. I point to the dirt just outside Silver Streak's stall.

"I found these heart-shaped hoofprints! They match the heart-bar horseshoes in Gwyneth's *Horse Girl's Veterinary Handbook*, which I found on the floor of the cabin, with a corner folded down to the page on laminitis."

"That's strange—none of the horses at Juniper Ranch have laminitis," Gwyneth says slowly. "The camp vet checked them all before we got here."

"Except for one," Clementine breathes.

We all flip our heads to her.

"OMG, that's right—Amara brought her *own* horse to camp!" Everleigh practically squeals.

"And the heart prints were in the stall *before* Silver Streak was taken!" I yelp. "Pasquale and I found them in the barn the night before he disappeared."

"Which means . . ." Noel paces back and forth, like a detective in one of her mystery novels. "Silver Streak had laminitis??"

A collective gasp goes up around the stall.

"Of course!" Gwyneth says excitedly. "That explains why Amara has been acting so strangely since we got to horse camp. She *knew* something was wrong with Silver Streak but didn't want to tell anyone. Because Silver Streak was definitely wearing regular horseshoes back at Oakwood, so the heart-bar shoes must have been put on right before he got to Juniper."

"Which explains why she brought Silver Streak to camp in the first place!" I say quickly. "She wanted to keep an eye on him to make sure he healed properly under her watch. She was trying to *protect* him."

My mind flashes back to the moment Amara let Bandit pass Silver Streak on our trail ride. It felt so strange at the time—Amara isn't exactly an "after you" kind of rider. Now I realize she was just trying to stop him from breaking into a trot.

"Poor Amara." Clementine shakes her head.

Noel peers over her glasses to inspect the hoofprints in the dirt. "She didn't tell any of us about *any* of this. She must have wanted to keep Silver Streak's injury a secret."

"Which means the horsenappers wouldn't know about it either!" The pieces fall together in my mind. "They would have assumed Silver Streak was still worth . . ."

"A million bucks," Everleigh says grimly, finishing my thought.

"Silver Streak could be in even *more* danger if they try to get him to jump or canter," Gwyneth warns.

"You're right," I say urgently. "We've got to get to them—now!"

"But where do we even start?" Noel sighs. "Mr. Gulch has been searching for days and hasn't found anything."

"Maybe that's the point?" I raise my eyebrows sharply, then point down to the hoofprints. "Let's follow those hearts!"

CHAPTER THIRTY-ONE

We quickly (and quietly) tug on our helmets, saddle our horses, and mount up inside the barn.

"Doesn't *anyone* think we should tell Nora or Mr. Gulch or one of the other counselors that Amara is missing?" Noel whimpers nervously.

"No," I say firmly. "The ransom note was clear on that. And Mr. Gulch warned us not to say anything to our parents. Which happens to be a *very* interesting coincidence. If we tell anyone, we could be putting Amara—and ourselves—in major danger."

"You just proved my point!" Noel says miserably.

"But why would Mr. Gulch steal Amara's horse?" Everleigh asks as she settles into Sierra's saddle. "He's been running this camp for years, and there's never been a horsenapping before."

"Juniper Ranch was never in danger of closing before,"

Gwyneth points out, adjusting Romeo's reins. "He might just be desperate enough for money that he'd try to sell a valuable horse to save the camp. Even if it didn't belong to him."

"But if he *doesn't* have anything to do with it, then we're all going to get in gigantic trouble for accusing him!" Noel cries from atop Tango. "And probably get kicked out of horse camp?!"

"Based on my astronomical timetables, we only have a few hours before the sun sets," Clementine says, glancing at her watch. "It's safer to go now than later."

"But—"

"You guys!" I snap. "Amara is our friend. Whether we're right or wrong, whether or not we risk getting kicked out, we need to help her. Every moment we waste is another moment she's in danger."

My eyes search theirs. Eventually, everyone nods in agreement.

I gently squeeze Bandit's rib cage, and he walks on, following the trail of hearts out the back of the barn.

Fortunately, it hasn't rained since Silver Streak disappeared. And while the drought may be terrible for the trees (and the mountain lions), it means his heart-bar hoofprints are still slightly visible in the dirt.

And since all of the counselors are still in the mess hall for their emergency meeting—fiercely debating exactly *who* is in charge of camp with Mr. Gulch away while we're supposedly "resting" in our cabin—we should have plenty of time to slip away in plain sight . . . without any of them noticing.

Our parade of horses *clip-clop*s down the main camp path away from the barn. We try to look as nonchalant as possible, like we're just regular old campers out for a regular old ride—instead of a ragtag group of rebels on a mission to save our friend.

Unfortunately, once we make it past the long row of cabins and to the edge of camp, the heart hoofprints seem to suddenly disappear.

Clementine leans over from her saddle and scans the ground below. "He must have turned into the forest."

"Oh, great!" Noel wails. "Now you expect us to walk right into the Forsaken Forest? Where we're never, *ever* supposed to go??"

"This is *not* a good idea," Everleigh agrees nervously.

Bandit and I move closer to a cluster of three aspens at the edge of the forest. I scan the ground furiously and—*there!* Just as I suspected, there's an indentation on the ground!

"The hearts head straight for the secret trail!"

"The secret what-now?" Everleigh asks.

"There's a secret trail in the forest!" The words rush from my mouth. "Amara and I took it the other day when we went for our bathroom break. She learned about it from Pasquale!

Who is also her secret brother?! Anyway, she said Mr. Gulch didn't know about the trail, but *of course* he must have. This is his ranch!"

"Whoa, whoa, slow down, Wills," Gwyneth repeats. "Amara has a secret brother?"

"And it's Pasquale?!" Everleigh scrunches her nose.

"I'll explain later!"

"I'm not sure if we're achieving synchronous clarity?" Clementine says.

Noel translates: "We have literally no idea what you're saying."

"This way!" I cry.

My tongue flicks out a *click-click*, and Bandit walks bravely ahead, through the thicket of ghostly burned trees that make up the Forsaken Forest. The other horses and their riders follow (reluctantly) behind, glancing nervously at the ominous branches that stretch down like bony fingers, warning us not to take another step.

But we *clip-clop* along the secret path anyway, searching frantically for more heart prints. Then suddenly, a sound in the forest stops us dead in our tracks.

"AHHHHHHHHHHHHHHHH!"

Chapter Thirty-Two

"AHHHHHHHHHHHHHHHH!"

"We've got to hurry!" I sit deep in my saddle and then squeeze my legs just behind the girth, collecting Bandit into a quick canter. We race ahead toward the scream.

Gwyneth calls after me as Bandit and I zoom ahead of the pack. "That sounds like—"

"Amara!" I spot her standing off the side of the trail, near the creepy, decrepit shack we found earlier this week. I tug hard on Bandit's reins. "Whoa, boy."

Fortunately, Bandit listens to me on the first try. He screeches to a halt, and I dismount in one fluid movement, quickly tying his reins to a splintery old post in front of the cabin.

I run the few steps to Amara. It's clear something has gone terribly wrong. Her face is twisted into an anguished grimace, and tears slide down her cheeks. "Are you okay??"

"Noooooo," she says, choking the syllables out through sobs. "Silver Streak . . . is . . . gone!"

"I know," I console her, wrapping an arm around her shoulder, which is still covered in the angry poison ivy rash. "We came to find you."

"No, you don't understand. He's *really* gone," she says, her eyes now wild.

Before I can ask what she means, the other Misty girls catch up to us, leaping down from their horses.

"Amara!" Gwyneth shouts.

"Are the kidnappers here?" Noel's voice quakes with fear as she notices the crumbling shack. "What even is this place?"

"Blink twice if we need to run!" Everleigh whispers urgently.

"The kidnappers?" Amara looks confused.

"We found this ransom note." I pull the slip of paper, covered with pasted-on magazine letters, from my breeches pocket. "When I couldn't find you in the infirmary, we assumed the horsenappers nabbed you as well."

"Have you seen them?" Gwyneth asks.

"Did they leave you and Silver Streak at this creepy place??" Noel's voice is still trembling.

"Are you okay?" Everleigh asks.

"I . . . no . . . I . . ." Amara's forehead crinkles, and she stammers through her tears. "I don't know where Silver Streak is."

"Everything's all right," Clementine says soothingly. "We're here now. You're safe."

Amara nods slowly, then shakes her head. "But Silver Streak isn't!" She buries her head in her hands, her glossy hair spilling over her face.

"How did you find me?" she mumbles through her fingers.

"We followed the heart prints," Noel explains.

"They led us to the secret trail," Everleigh adds.

"You know about the secret trail?" Amara asks, shooting me a look.

"Amara?" Gwyneth says softly. "We figured out your other secret, too."

"You did?!" Amara jerks upright. "I mean—what other secret?"

"We know Silver Streak has laminitis," I answer. "We figured out he was wearing special heart-bar shoes, to help him heal. We're guessing you didn't tell anyone because you were so worried about him—you were just trying to protect him. And that's probably why you decided to bring him to camp. So you could take care of him."

Amara's eyes flick between our faces.

"Wow, I . . . I can't believe you figured it out. You're . . ." She swallows, like she's gathering her strength. "Really good friends. To come looking for me."

Then, surprisingly, she smiles. "It's almost like I have my

own personal Sherlock Holmes! Or should I say . . . Sherlock *Horse*?"

The rest of us exchange glances—Amara seems to be glitching. She'd never in a million years make a terrible dad joke like that. (Or utter any phrase that I might also bedazzle on a T-shirt.) Poor Amara, the stress must really be getting to her.

"We're so sorry Silver Streak is hurt," Noel says.

Amara's head whips around. "He's going to be *fine*?"

"Of *course* he is," Clem says gently, like she's talking to a rabid bear.

"We just need to find him," Amara whimpers. "Before tomorrow!"

"We *will*," Gwyneth reassures her. "The Oakwood Flyers would never let you down."

"And neither would I," Clementine adds.

"Did you follow the horsenappers to this creepy place?" Everleigh asks.

"Not exactly." Amara squints, recounting the afternoon.

"I snuck out of the infirmary so I could get my face lotion from the cabin. Because, as some of you may or may not know"—she looks pointedly at me—"it's really important to stick with a twice-daily skincare routine? Before I left, I piled a bunch of pillows in my infirmary cot to make it look like I was sleeping. That way Mrs. Hailey wouldn't worry if she woke up and I wasn't there. But when I got to Misty, I found the ransom note on my bunk! I knew I had to do something, since Mr. Gulch is *completely* incompetent?? But after I read the note, I *also* knew I couldn't ask anyone for help. So I decided to take matters into my own hands. I followed the heart-bar prints down the secret trail and ended up here—just like you. They end at the shack, but . . . as you can see . . . there's no sign of Silver Streak anywhere."

"I'm so sorry." Everleigh shakes her head. "We were hoping we'd find him, too."

"I wish we could have come with you in the first place," Gwyneth adds. "But at least we're together now."

"Actually?" Clementine looks up. "We should all probably head back to camp soon. It'll be dark in just a couple of hours, and there's a nasty storm coming."

"How can you tell, Clem?" Gwyneth glances up at the cloudless blue sky.

"I fell off my horse last year at the LA Spring Classic and broke my wrist. Now it always starts aching before a storm arrives," Clementine explains. "It's like my own personal weather vane!"

"I'm not leaving," Amara says adamantly. "Not without Silver Streak."

"But the emergency counselor meeting will be over soon," Everleigh yelps. "Nora's going to notice if we're all missing. And she'll probably call the police?"

Noel's eyes grow as big as Tango's. "The police *definitely* count as adults!"

Ugh. My mind toggles between all of our terrible choices,

trying to decide on the least-terrible option. I once again desperately wish someone would just tell me what to do. Like my parents . . . or Kay . . . or Nora . . . or Georgia . . . or Clyde Lee . . . or, I don't know, Dolly Parton?!

But I know none of them are here right now. So I'm going to have to put on my big-girl breeches, sprinkle some magic fairy grit, and figure this out myself.

"I'll stay with Amara."

Ten heads (five human and five horse) flip around to face me.

"The two of us can look for Silver Streak while the rest of you go back to the cabin and distract Nora," I explain, carefully laying out my plan. "We'll come back to Misty before dark. Hopefully with an extra horse."

The Claremont triplets and Clementine trade worried glances, while Amara actually looks grateful. (Whoa, so *that's* what Amara's face looks like when she doesn't detest me!)

"I really don't have a good feeling about us splitting up . . ." Gwyneth sighs. "But it may be our only choice."

CHAPTER THIRTY-THREE

Click-click. Click-click. Click-click. Click-click.

Amara and I help Gwyneth, Everleigh, Noel, and Clementine mount up, then watch as the foursome and their horses head back down the secret trail toward camp.

Once they disappear from view, there's an awkward pause.

"So, um, how's your poison ivy?" I ask cheerfully, pointing to the red splotches on Amara's arms in a bizarre attempt to make conversation.

"It's fine??" she says. "We should get moving."

"Right." *Ugh, Willa, you're supposed to be finding Silver Streak, not discussing wilderness rashes!* "You can ride on Bandit with me. He's strong enough to carry us both."

"That would be amazing." Amara pauses sheepishly. "Actually? Let me take a quick bathroom break first. I can't believe this shack doesn't have a powder room." Then she sulks off into a thick patch of trees, far away from the cabin.

As I wait for her, I check on Bandit, who's still tied to the crumbling wooden post.

"You okay, boy?" I ask, stroking his forelock. "You're so brave to keep us company at this creepy place."

He *pfffffft*s proudly.

But as I reach down to untie him, I notice something shiny lying on top of his post.

"You forgot your . . . ," I call after Amara, but she's already out of earshot.

I don't mean to look (I swear!), but there's a photo open on Amara's phone. And it's of the ransom note . . .

I zoom in closer. How odd. Why would Amara take a photo of the ransom note instead of bringing it with her? Now that I think about it, she left the *real* note out on her bunk in Misty . . . where anyone could have easily found it. Was she hoping that we—*or someone else?*—would discover it and come looking for her?

I pull the actual ransom note from my pocket to read it again. And that's when I notice it . . . a splatter of pink paint, glowing from the corner of the page.

"Well, that was disgusting!"

Amara's footsteps crunch closer. I shove the note in my pocket and carefully set her phone back on the post, exactly where I found it.

"Amara? I think I know who took your horse."

"You do??" Her eyes go wide.

"This isn't easy to say, but I think—"

"It's Mr. Gulch! It *has* to be him," Amara blurts. "He just wants to sell Silver Streak to get money to save his camp! He's hated me from day one for bringing my horse to—"

"It's your brother!" I interrupt. "I ran into Pasquale at the Craft Shack earlier today. He was standing right next to the art-supply cabinet when I came inside, and he seemed to be out of breath, like he'd just run from somewhere. When I mentioned the pink Pony Paint was missing, he started acting really strangely. And blinking! Then I found this splash of pink Pony Paint on the ransom note."

I carefully unfold the paper to show her the smudge. "See? It's a thumbprint in the exact same shade of pink." I lick my finger and dampen the paint splotch, which quickly fades away. "And see how it washes off easily as soon as it gets wet, just like chalk Pony Paint? It's so obvious—whoever took the Pony Paint must have also made this letter. As much as my neckerchief-loving heart doesn't want to admit it, I caught Pasquale right at the scene of the crime."

"Wait, this doesn't make any sense—"

"Amara, think about it! Pasquale probably knew *exactly* how valuable Silver Streak is from your dad. Or maybe he was just trying to play a really mean practical joke on his new stepsister? But either way—"

Plop.

A huge drop of rain falls onto Amara's shoulder, startling both of us.

Plop-plop-plop.

The droplets begin to tumble down harder.

I look over and see a stream of pink lines running down Amara's hands and arms.

"Amara . . . are you bleeding?"

She looks down at her skin, now awash in ribbons of bubble-gum-colored water.

My thoughts tangle, and I feel short of breath, like I can't figure out which way is up to find a gulp of air. And then, suddenly, it hits me.

Amara's rash isn't poison ivy . . .

It's Pony Paint.

Pink Pony Paint.

CHAPTER THIRTY-FOUR

"You gave yourself fake poison ivy? Using *Pony Paint*??"

"I—I . . . ," Amara stammers helplessly, looking down at the pink streaks on her arms.

My brain twists as I realize I just caught Amara red—make that *pink*—handed. But what I can't figure out is . . . *whyyyyyyy*?

Why would someone—especially someone who's as completely obsessed with her skin as Amara—invent an itchy, disgusting rash? Especially when it meant she'd miss the best-ever day of horse camp (i.e., creek swimming)? Was she trying to hide something from us? Or—whoa—hide *someone* from us??

My body suddenly floods with adrenaline.

OMG.

Ohhh 👏 emmm 👏 geeee 👏.

"*You* wrote the ransom note?!?!"

Amara looks down guiltily. But I notice her stealing a side glance over my shoulder, toward the creepy cabin.

I whip my head around, following her gaze. I steel my courage, tug my trusty flashlight from my pocket, and venture through the doorframe, which is leaning precariously to one side. I sweep the beam of light across the dark, spooky shack—then freeze when it lands on a shadowy pile in the corner of the room.

It's all there . . . the huge pile of hay, the beautiful leather saddle, and, yep, the box of NickerDoodles. I snatch the box and run back outside the cabin, holding it in the air like I just found a prize in my cereal.

"*You* were the one who brought Silver Streak here, weren't you?" I gasp as the missing puzzle pieces snap into place in my mind. "You knew he'd feel safer with his favorite snack, didn't you? No random horsenappers would know about the NickerDoodles!"

I emphasize each point with a shake of the gourmet cookie box. Bandit's ears perk up from his post outside the cabin. He knows the sound of tasty snacks when he hears them!

"You accused *me* of leaving the paddock door open and letting Silver Streak wander off, but *you* took him!" I continue. "And you brought his saddle to ride him for exercise, and plenty of hay so he wouldn't go hungry."

Her lips tremble, and she looks down at the ground again.

"*Why*, Amara? Why would you scare all of us like this? We

thought you were *kidnapped*! By creepy horsenappers! We thought we were putting our *lives* at risk to help you!"

I know I'm spiraling, but the words won't stop flinging from my mouth.

"Is this your idea of a sick joke? Blaming me and almost getting me kicked out of horse camp? Then inventing imaginary thieves? And staying silent when I blamed your sweet, brill— I mean, *innocent* brother? And Clementine. And the Claremont triplets. And that poor ghost horse! Not to mention Nora and Mr. Gulch. They've been nothing but kind and generous to me. And to you! How could you lie to all of us like this, Amara??"

My eyes narrow, daring her to answer.

But just as Amara opens her mouth to speak, her phone lights up. I lunge to grab it before she can, knocking over the box of NickerDoodles in the process. I lift the phone in the air just as a message pops up on the lock screen.

MOM

> Silver Streak's been horsenapped?!? 🐴 ✖

> The very day before we were going to file the insurance claim policy?? 😮 😮

> I can't believe I let your father convince me to sign you up for this tacky camp. We will sue for negligence! 😠 ⛺

I'll have insurance agent meet me @ Juniper tomorrow to investigate. No need to call police. If SS truly horsenapped, v. v. sad and awful.

But also? Could solve all our problems?? 🐴🐴

CHAPTER THIRTY-FIVE

"Give me that!" Amara cries.

I stretch the phone higher in the air with my extra-long arms.

"Not until you explain *everything*, Amara," I demand, my voice low with fury. "The *truth* this time."

Bandit tilts his head curiously at us. He can't understand what silly game of keep-away we're playing.

"Okay," she eventually whimpers. "I did it. I took Silver Streak."

The rain that's been pummeling us suddenly pauses—as if even Mother Nature can't believe that Amara would actually betray her favorite horse . . . and her supposed forever friends.

"Because my mom was going to trade him in!"

Bandit snorts as my eyebrows crumple in confusion. "What do you mean?"

"Silver Streak was *really* expensive. So my mom took

out an insurance policy on him? She said that way if he got injured or sick in the first three years we had him, she could *exchange* him and get the insurance money for a new horse."

Amara shakes her head in disbelief.

"That's how she said it, Willa—*exchange* him. Like he was an Hermès bag with a defect!"

I consider explaining to Amara that the only designer bags I'm familiar with are the ones that hold oats. But I desperately want her to keep talking, so I nod sympathetically. "Ugh, I hate when that happens."

"Me too," she sniffles. "But Silver Streak isn't just some gorgeous leather accessory with an unfortunate blemish. He's my best friend in the entire world! And he loves me—unconditionally. My mom, on the other hand, only cares about me when I'm bringing home blue ribbons."

I try to process everything Amara's telling me, but my mind is spinning.

"Amara, I know your mom can be, um . . . *challenging*. But I also know she loves you. *And* Silver Streak. This must be some sort of mix—"

But Amara cuts me off.

"No, Wills—you're wrong."

She takes a deep breath.

"We found out Silver Streak had laminitis before camp. Fortunately, we caught it really, really early. But my mom *still* called the insurance company. She said he was no good to us anymore—that he'd never recover enough to compete as a professional jumper. Even though Silver Streak finished all his medicine and the vet said he was doing amazing! She put those special heart-bar shoes on him to be safe and said we just needed to give him some time to heal. But my mom said we couldn't wait around on a horse that may or may not be able to jump again. She said we have to start thinking *seriously* about my career if I want to make it to a good college jumping program and then to the Olympics someday."[1]

Amara's pacing back and forth, almost like she's in a trance.

"But I convinced her to let me bring Silver Streak to Juniper Ranch for one last adventure together. She agreed, since the insurance paperwork would take a while to process. I figured it was my only chance to buy enough time to save him. I just couldn't imagine losing him."

Her eyes glisten with tears.

"That's why you didn't want me to see your phone," I say gently. "I assumed you were just watching HorseTube or posting outfit pics of your cute pink breeches. I had no idea you were trying to convince your mom to let you keep Silver Streak."

"I didn't want anyone to know what was happening until

---

[1] Unlike most athletic events, men and women compete directly against each other in equestrian events—and so do male and female horses. In fact, it's one of the few Olympic sports that's not split into separate men's and women's divisions. We're all just riders, plain and simple.

I had a plan," she explains. "Although . . . I did also post some pics of my breeches?"

I raise an eyebrow.

"They were super cute!"

"But what does any of this have to do with taking your own horse??"

"I'm getting there! After my mom's text, I remembered one crucial fact. Our insurance policy also covers *stolen* horses. Which means . . . if Silver Streak was horsenapped, my mom would still get the insurance money to buy a new jumper. But we wouldn't have to give Silver Streak back. Because you can't give back a horse who's been, you know, horsenapped!"

My eyes go wide.

"But wouldn't the horse who's horsenapped also be, um . . . *horsenapped*??"

"Yes! Which would be a very big problem. *Unless* . . . you horsenapped him yourself." Amara takes a little bow of victory.

"But how did you nap him? And where? And when??"

"I waited until the dead of night—once you and Nora and everyone in Misty were all fast asleep. It was right after you came back from your little late-night adventure at the barn."

"Wait, you heard me?"

"Of course I heard you, I'm an extremely elegant sleeper," she says primly. "Plus, Pasquale told me. Anyway, once I heard you join Nora facing off in the Snoring Olympics, I slipped away to the barn, quickly saddled up Silver Streak, and rode him down the secret trail to the shack. I got him all settled in with plenty of hay and water and NickerDoodles."

I lean down to scoop up the cookies that scattered on the ground after I dropped the box. "Wait, you already knew about the shack? I thought we found it together?"

She gives me a *try-to-keep-up* eye roll. "Of *course* I did. My bathroom emergency on the trail was just an excuse so I could make sure it was big enough to stash Silver Streak!"

"Wow, you really are an evil genius," I say, shaking my head.

"Thank you!" She smiles proudly.

"But why did you blame *me* for Silver Streak disappearing?"

"I had no idea you were going to confess to possibly leaving the stall door and the paddock gate open. Because—news flash—you absolutely *didn't* leave the door or the gate open! Your meltdown was just a major bonus. I went along with it to create a distraction, so that no one would suspect me. But I swear, Wills, I never meant to get you in trouble."

The funny thing is? I actually believe her.

"I knew that if Mr. Gulch thought Silver Streak had bolted, he'd search the neighboring ranches . . . no matter how far away. But Silver Streak was right under everybody's noses all along . . . tucked safe and sound inside a cozy shack in the Forsaken Forest."

"And *then* what were you going to do with him?"

"Um, borrow some black Pony Paint to disguise his white star?" she says sheepishly. "I thought maybe when I eventually brought him home, nobody would know it was actually him?"

"What about the first time you gave him a bath??"

"I don't know—it was *not* a perfect plan!" Amara takes another deep breath.

"In the meantime, I had to find a way to keep sneaking out of Misty so I could take care of Silver Streak. That's when I came up with the idea for the fake poison ivy. It was much easier to slip out from the infirmary with that old nurse snoozing all the time.

"I borrowed *The Horse Girl's Veterinary Handbook* from Gwyneth's bunk so I could monitor Silver Streak's recovery, and the *HORSENAPPED!* novel from Noel's shelf so I could figure out how to write a ransom note. I knew the insurance company would need some sort of proof he was stolen."

"But I found those books under *Nora's* bed," I point out.

"I heard you coming back to the cabin and didn't have time to put them back. So I kicked them under Nora's bed to keep everyone off my trail!"

"It worked," I sigh, cringing that I ever suspected sweet Nora of stealing a camper's horse to help her stunt-riding career.

"Then I trimmed off a bit of Silver Streak's mane, braided it, and attached it to the note," Amara continues. "I thought if it looked like one of the cut-off horse tails from Mr. Gulch's ghorst story, it would confuse everybody even more."

"Mission accomplished!" I congratulate her. "Wait a minute, you cut off his *real* mane?"

"I had to make it look convincing!" she says defensively. "Fortunately, if anyone can pull off side bangs, it's Silver Streak."

Bandit tosses his flaxen mane in agreement.

"But I made one fatal mistake," Amara confesses. "I didn't realize I'd left that pink splotch on the ransom note. I'd just freshened up my poison ivy rash, so I guess the Pony Paint was still wet. Nobody in the world would have noticed that tiny detail except for you, Wills."

I beam triumphantly at my successful detective work, before returning to Amara's tangled tale.

"So you horsenapped Silver Streak . . . because it was the only way you could think of to save him . . . from *your mom*?"

"Exactly!" Amara exhales, and her shoulders relax, free from the heavy weight of the secret she's been carrying all alone. "I love him so much, Willa."

An urgent desperation creeps back into her voice. "But my mom can never know any of this! She'd probably trade *me* in if she found out."

I glance up at the sky, where more storm clouds have begun to gather.

"You have my word as an Oakwood Flyer," I promise. "But

the four of us—you, me, Bandit, and Silver Streak—have to get back to camp. The rain is going to start again any minute, and it's way too dangerous to be here alone after dark."

"No, Willa, you didn't let me finish." Amara grips my hand. "Silver Streak is *really* gone this time."

CHAPTER THIRTY-SIX

"What do you mean he's *really* gone this time?" I ask, throwing my hands up in frustration. "You just told me you brought him here to the shack!"

"I did!"

"So let's get his saddle on him and go home! Is he tied up behind the cabin?"

"Not anymore! When I came by this afternoon to bring him fresh hay, after I snuck out of the infirmary? He was gone."

Amara points helplessly to the ground near the fence where Bandit is tied.

"I found the rope I'd been using as a halter lying on the ground. At first I thought he'd been taken by *real* horsenappers, but—"

She looks at her cell phone, which I'm still holding above my head. I glance up at it as well.

"Wait—are you making this all up and recording me for a hilarious HorseTube video? Is that why I found your phone on the fence??" Amara's story is full of so many twists and turns at this point that it *has* to be a cruel practical joke.

"No, I swear! I set my phone up to record Silver Streak while I was gone, to keep an eye on him," she explains. "When I came back and realized he was gone, I assumed the worst—that a mountain lion or some *real* horse thieves had snatched him. But when I checked the recording, it was just Silver Streak pulling a Houdini. He slipped out of his halter and galloped off on his own!"

I stare at her in shock, my mouth hanging open.

"So you're telling me . . . first you horsenapped your own horse? And then your horse horsenapped *himself*??"

She pauses for a moment, then nods. "I guess that pretty much sums it up."

My face tightens into a worried grimace. "Ugh, Silver Streak probably felt the storm coming and got scared—or went looking for you."

"Wills, he's somewhere in this forest, all alone. We've got to find him before . . ."

"Before the mountain lions do," I finish with a gulp.

She nods grimly as Bandit whinnies at the cell phone, skittering backward. (It's a small, shiny object so naturally he assumes it wants to murder him!)

I give Bandit a soothing pat to calm him, then turn to

Amara, forcing myself to sound brave. "Come on. Let's go find your boy."

We hastily gather a few supplies: my flashlight, some bottles of water, a length of rope to serve as a makeshift halter, and—our secret weapon—the NickerDoodles.

Amara and I help each other mount up onto Bandit's saddle, which is still damp and slippery from the rain. I sit in front (for once!) on the saddle, while Amara rides bareback behind me, hugging my waist.

I flick my tongue into a *click-click* and gently squeeze my knees. Bandit dutifully sets off down the secret trail—deeper into the Forsaken Forest.

Chapter Thirty-Seven

The sun slips lower, threatening to sink behind the mountain that looms over Juniper Ranch. With little time to waste, we hurry down the trail, riding double on Bandit and searching desperately for any signs of Silver Streak.[1]

"Any heart prints?" Amara asks hopefully from behind me.

"No." I sigh heavily. "Not a heart in sight. Maybe he wandered off the secret path and threaded his way through the scorched trees?"

"Ugh, I wish he'd just left us a note telling us where he'd gone," she sighs. "But we have to keep looking."

We continue down the secret path, which grows steeper

---

[1] Two riders + one horse = riding double. The person in the back of this equation should always be an experienced, confident equestrian, who avoids sitting on the horse's kidneys or squeezing the flank area and startling him. You never want to go too fast while riding double in case your horse is thrown off balance. Imagine trying to carry two of your friends piggyback at the same time!

as we venture deeper into the forest. I scan the ground on either side of the trail, letting Bandit pick out his own path. I remind myself that he doesn't want to stumble any more than we do. *Especially* with two riders on his back.

"I just don't see—"

Heeeeeeeeeeeeeeeeeeeee!

A squeal rings out in the distance. Bandit screeches to a stop and lets out a frightened whinny in reply.

"That sounds like Silver Streak!" Amara cries. "He must be in trouble!"

Heeeeeeeeeeeeeeeeeeeee!

Another horse squeal echoes up through the canyon. Bandit tosses his head in the air, then takes a few scattered steps backward.

"Easy, boy," I call to Bandit. "I know that's a scary sound, but we've got to stay calm."

My brave soldier, however, is clearly terrified—he has no interest whatsoever in moving forward or calming down.

"We have to keep going," Amara pleads, instinctively leaning forward and adding pressure with her legs. "Silver Streak must be close!"

But the squeeze from Amara seems to upset Bandit even more. He pops his front feet a few inches off the ground, then throws his head up again.

"He's about to rear!" I warn Amara. "Hang on!"

Amara thrusts her arms around my waist, clutching her hands together.

But it's too late. Bandit has already committed to his dangerous revolt. He leans his weight on his back legs, flicks his tail furiously, then explodes his front legs high into the air, leaning back so he's practically vertical.

Aaaaaaah!!!

I slide backward in the saddle—still slick from the earlier rain—pressing hard against Amara. I squeeze my knees tightly into Bandit's sides and try to hang on.

But Amara, behind me, can't quite get a grip. As Bandit flings us backward and kicks higher into the air, her arms lose their grasp around me and she slips sideways, tumbling to the ground.

"Aaaaah!" she cries again, as she rolls away from Bandit to protect herself.

I desperately want to shriek but force myself to stay quiet. If Bandit hears me panicking, he'll rear again. I need to get him under control if I want to keep us all safe.

I lean forward, into his neck, trying to keep myself centered in the saddle. I make sure to give him plenty of rein—I don't want to tug his head back any farther—he could lose his balance and fall back on top of me!

"Whoa, whoaaaah," I keep repeating calmly. "Easy, easy."

I'm surprised to hear the voice coming out of my mouth sound so reassured. (Especially when my inside voice is panic-screaming!)

But after a few more terrifying seconds, Bandit listens to my commands, finally landing back on earth. He snorts as I circle him around a few times until he eventually cools down.

"Amara, are you all right??" I glance around and find her standing on the side of the trail, hopping on one foot.

"My ankle," she whimpers. "I think I twisted it."

"I'm going to dismount and get you back up on Bandit. He's calmed down now. You can ride, and I'll lead you both back to camp on my own two feet."

Amara winces as she tries to put weight on her ankle. "There's no way I can mount up. You have to keep going without me."

She inhales sharply through gritted teeth, and a look of pain shoots across her face.

"I'll canter back to camp as quick as I can and get help."

"No," she says tightly through her grimace. "You have to keep looking!"

"Amara, I'm not leaving you in the woods in the dark with a twisted ankle and a massive storm coming!"

"Please?" she begs. "We're so close, Willa. I *know* that squeal was him. You still have a few minutes of daylight to find more heart prints—and save Silver Streak."

I shake my head—but her eyes plead with me again.

"Please?" she whispers softly. "I would do it for you."

I think about all the A Secret Friend notes of encouragement Amara helped write for me back at Oakwood Riding Academy. And the way she saved my heart-horse, Clyde Lee, from being sold. And how she convinced her mom to create a scholarship for me this summer. And all the millions of other ways she's quietly, miraculously helped me over the last year.

Amara's telling the truth. She absolutely *would* do this for me.

"Okay," I nod. "I'll keep looking, but only for a few minutes. I don't want to leave you alone for long."

I hand back her phone (which still, incredibly, has a few bars of signal) and a bottle of water from Bandit's saddlebag. She passes me Dad's flashlight, which I tuck snugly into my pocket.

"Thank you, Wills." Tears fill Amara's eyes. "And BTW? I'm not crying because my ankle hurts? I'm crying because—"

"I know," I say gently.

And then Bandit and I set off.

Chapter Thirty-Eight

My hands cling tightly to Bandit's reins as we bound down the forest path, his swift hooves carrying us farther away from Juniper Ranch.

Galumph, galumph, ga—booooooooom.

Bandit's ears swivel back, and he screeches to a halt. A deep rumble growls in the distance and the sky darkens.

"There's no reason to be nervous, boy," I say, the words tumbling out of my mouth.

I scan the ground around us with the flashlight my dad forced me to pack. Sweeping the beam of light across the trail, I search frantically for the hoofprints I *know* must be nearby.

"Yes, I know we're not supposed to leave camp. Especially after dark. Especially alone. Especially without telling anyone. *Especially*—"

BAAA-BOOOOM!!

We both nearly leap out of our skin as a deafening clap of thunder rattles across the canyon. I feel the muscles in Bandit's neck tense; he paws at the ground as his ears prick sharply forward, like a bull's—all sure signs he's about to spook. I lean forward to stroke his crest, trying to soothe him.

"Especially when a storm might be coming," I breathe, attempting once again to sound calm. (Even though I absolutely, positively do *not* feel calm!) I tuck my flashlight away, then steal a glance at the herd of clouds that are now stampeding across the full moon.

"Look, those thunderheads are still on the other side of the mountain," I say, forcing my voice into a cheerful, *everything-is-totally-under-control* register. "We've got plenty of time to find that horse and make it back safe and sound before—"

CRACK!!!

A burst of lightning explodes like fireworks above the canopy of pine trees that tower over us.

"Before anyone notices we're gone," I finish, swallowing hard. "Okay, so maybe the storm is getting a *teeny-tiny* bit closer? Have I mentioned I am *not* a meteorologist??"

I look down to see Bandit's reins trembling in my clammy hands. It appears that *I* am now the one who needs soothing. I take a deep breath of the suffocatingly heavy air, hoping to slow my galloping heart. Then I let out a *click-click* to get him moving again.

But Bandit pulls hard at his reins, skittering sideways and attempting to make a U-turn back toward home.

"Come on, boy," I grunt, nudging his ribs and battling him in a tug-of-war. "I know you want your bag of oats just as much as I want my midnight s'mores. But if we don't move quickly, the storm will wash away those hoofprints—and our only chance of finding our friend!"

Bandit flings his head back longingly to the safety of camp and his cozy stall. But before he can bolt, we both hear the sickening, high-pitched squeal of a horse in the distance.

Heeeeeeeeeeeee!!!

"He's in serious danger!" I plead, my voice turning raspy as I fight the panic growing inside me.

Bandit squeals back—then threatens to rear again! I begin to lose my balance. The flashlight in my hand waves wildly through the air as I try to steady myself. And then the bouncing beam of light lands on something . . . just ahead of us on the trail . . .

A heart-shaped hoofprint.

Chapter Thirty-Nine

I manage to calm Bandit before he rears again, then shine my flashlight down the trail of heart prints. They seem to lead from the secret path toward Juniper Creek Run. *Of course!* Silver Streak must have gotten thirsty and wandered off to look for a drink!

Just like the mountain lions. (Gulp.)

I try to coax Bandit onto the steep creek trail, but he remains frozen in place, still unnerved by the thunder. I reach into his saddlebag for a NickerDoodle, stretching it toward his lips. Fortunately, he gobbles down the bribe.

"You can have all the NickerDoodles in the world if you do this for me, boy," I beg. "Just please, *please* keep moving."

The promise of fancy snacks seems to soothe Bandit, and he shifts into gear, stepping confidently ahead through the moonlight. We follow the heart prints down the trail's perilously steep switchbacks toward Juniper Creek—and the sickening squealing we heard earlier.

As we reach the smooth rocks near the creek bank, my mind flashes back to our sunny Horseback Swim yesterday. Everything felt so magical then—like nothing bad could ever possibly happen in this place. But now that I'm here all alone? With the moonlight playing hide-and-seek with the storm clouds? And a creek full of dangerous, rushing water just a few steps away?

It's absolutely terrifying.

I take a few deep breaths and try to chase the looming weather from my mind. Then I remind myself that my friends (both the human kind and the horse kind) are counting on me. I *need* to focus.

Silver Streak. We're here to find Silver Streak.

I swipe my flashlight across the top of the creek—and find nothing but blackness. The water sounds even louder than before, like someone's cranked up the faucet to full blast.

"Must be pouring on the other side of the mountain," I mumble to myself.

I try sweeping the flashlight again. And this time? A glimmer of light reflects back to me. I blink furiously as my vision adjusts to the growing darkness.

Is that . . . an eye? A large, beautiful eye? Attached to a large, shadowy figure? Who has lowered his long, elegant, *magnificent* neck to lap up a drink of water from the creek?!

SILVER STREAK!!!!

I'd recognize that white star on his forehead and glossy black coat anywhere! I'm dying to scream out, *WE FOUND HIM!!!!*

But I don't want to startle Silver Streak, especially when I'm *this close* to catching him. "Easy, boy," I say softly, as Bandit nickers a friendly hello to his pal.

Silver Streak replies with an underwater snort—he's trying to decide whether to trust us or not.

"We're here to bring you home to Amara," I explain.

Silver Streak stops, mid-sip, to look up at us. He glances curiously at Bandit, then turns his gaze to me, blinking his beautiful eyelashes several times before taking another deep drink and snorting more bubbles.

He's clearly less than impressed that it took us so long to find him.

But—ohhh 👏 emmm 👏 geeee 👏! We *found* him!!!

I pinch myself to keep from squealing with excitement.

"You must be thirsty after all that walking, boy," I say, keeping my tone slow and even. Silver Streak has no lead or saddle or anything else for me to grab. The only way I'm going to keep him standing still for the moment is with my calmest, gentlest voice.

"Would it be okay if Bandit and I joined you for a sip?"

Silver Streak just keeps slurping, as if to say, *You do you, girl.*

"I'm going to dismount now," I say softly. "Stay right where you are, buddy."

I move in slow motion, deliberately lifting my gangly right leg over the saddle, then carefully lowering myself down Bandit's side.

Bandit's hooves make a satisfying *clop-clop* sound over the smooth rocks as I lead him toward the edge of the creek. Silver Streak looks up at us again, but he makes no sign of moving from his spot.

Once we reach the water, Bandit sticks his face in the water next to Silver Streak and glugs with abandon. It's like the creek is their own gigantic Stanley cup.

"Not all in one drink, Bandit!" I whisper-giggle. "I guess all those scary things on the trail today made you thirsty, too."

As both horses gulp away, I oh-so-slowly reach into the bag attached to Bandit's saddle, gingerly uncoiling the rope I brought with me from the shack . . . along with two NickerDoodles.

I slip the cookies in my pocket, then loosen the knot on the rope, creating an extra-large loop. I take a breath, inching closer to Silver Streak.

"Easy, boys," I murmur. I'm now close enough to gently stroke Silver Streak's star. I notice a large chunk of his mane is missing, where Amara lopped it off for the ransom note.

(She's right—Silver Streak really can rock side bangs like nobody's business.)

I move my hand slowly down his crest and mane until I reach his shoulders. But just as I'm about to gently toss the rope around his neck—

BA-BOOOM!!

Another earsplitting clap of thunder crackles across the creek.

Both Silver Streak and Bandit prick up their ears and swivel them around toward the sound. They snort nervously. My hands grow sweaty with panic as it registers that one—*or both!*—of them is about to bolt.

BOOOOOOOOOM!

The rumble is longer this time, and I feel Silver Streak's muscles tense under my palm.

Do something, Willa! my brain orders. I glance down at my GRIT bracelet—and realize I have only one option.

The moment Silver Streak starts to move, I skip along next to him, instinctively grabbing a chunk of his choppy mane with my left hand and his back with my right. I use all my strength to spring off the ground, then heave myself up and over his body.

And this time? Instead of face-planting in the dirt? I feel myself land squarely on his back! Holy #HorseGirl, I think I just pulled off my first running mount. *Bareback!*

"I've got you," I whisper giddily to Silver Streak as a grin explodes across my face. I wish I had Clementine's telepathy (or, you know, an actual phone!) so I could tell Amara that her boy is safe. And everyone else that I just aced a running mount!

"You've got to slow down so you don't hurt yourself," I warn Silver Streak, hoping he doesn't take off on a joy ride while I'm clinging on for dear life without a saddle. "You're only supposed to be walking right now. So I'm going to hitch you to Bandit's lead and stroll you both back to camp."

But as I lean forward on Silver Streak's back, stretching my hand toward Bandit's reins—

Craaaaaaaaaaaack!

Lightning explodes above us, and a torrent of rain cascades down from the sky.

Now it's Bandit's turn. *(Ugh!)* He whinnies loudly, then takes off, bolting in fear through the pounding rain—with his reins dangling dangerously down from his bit.

"Bandit, no!" I cry, pleading with him to stop. *(Exactly how many horses can a girl lose in one week??)*

But with no rider on board, fear overtakes my sweet soldier. He careens dangerously into the deep, rushing water of the creek, which seems to be moving even faster now. Soon he's swimming with only his head above water. I'm terrified that his reins will tangle in his front legs—or on a rock at the bottom of the creek, trapping him underwater.

Bandit horse-paddles farther down the now-gushing stream, then attempts to paw his way back up the muddy bank. But the rain is still pouring, and the bank is growing slipperier by the second. My poor boy can't find a hoof-hold! He could trip on his loose reins any second . . . and slide back into the churning water, which is now swirling with dangerous whirlpools.

"*Bandit!!!*" I call out in anguish.

Then, out of the darkness, comes a deep, steady voice.

"*Whoaaaah,*" it commands.

And Bandit, miraculously, freezes.

CHAPTER FORTY

"*Whoaaaaa.*" The voice is calm and cool—and familiar? "That's it, Bandit. I've got you."

She appears like an apparition from the forest, riding on a very petite pony, calmly gathering Bandit's reins in her hands and leading him safely up the creek bank.

"Amara?!" I gasp.

"Silver Streak!" she cries, ignoring me to beam at the beautiful black jumper beneath me. He whinnies a loud, relieved hello at her sight.

"I was afraid I'd never see you again!" Amara coaxes Macaroni and Bandit closer to us so she can stroke Silver Streak's muzzle. He buries his face in her (amazingly still glossy) hair, nickering with relief.

I reach over to rub Bandit's soaking-wet neck. "This is why we never swim alone, boy!"

We make an unlikely crew: three horses, two girls, one big rainstorm, and way too many emotions to count.

Eventually, Amara looks up at me, her eyes damp with gratitude. "You saved him, Wills."

"And you saved me," I say. "Not to mention Bandit."

She shrugs from atop Macaroni, like she rescues runaway horses (and novice #HorseGirls) every day. But then her tears spill over.

"I'm sorry I've been acting strangely this summer," she blubbers. "Besides the whole I'm-losing-my-heart-horse thing and the whole my-dad-moved-away-and-I-suddenly-have-a-brother thing, I guess I was a little jealous that you became friends with all the Oakwood Flyers, plus Clementine *and* Pasquale so easily. I've never been good at that."

"Wait, what?" I say, dumbfounded. "You're the Queen of the #HorseGirls, Amara. Everyone worships you!"

"But is it for the right reasons?" she sniffles, genuinely pondering the question. "If someone is *your* friend, you know they like you for you. It's obviously not for, like, your expensive clothes."

"Right," I nod, glancing down at the filthy TAIL-OR SWIFT FAN CLUB shirt I am still rocking.

"But I'm never sure if people like me for me or for my mom's bank account. Or, you know, my amazing eyebrows?"

"They *are* pretty amazing," I say, smiling archly, "but I promise you I'm not your friend because of your stunning facial hair."

I manage to coax a giggle out of Amara. "The point is?" she continues. "If I'm ever acting strange, it's probably just something weird going on in my brain. Or, like, my mom trying to give my horse away. It's not because I don't think you're low-key amazing."

"You can always tell me if something hard is going on in your life, Amara. I'll always try to help." And then, I can't help it, I bend down from Silver Streak to try to hug her.

"Eeek, Wills! You're all *muddy*?!" She laughs and shoos Macaroni and Bandit away from my long reach.

I like to imagine this is Amara's way of saying, *We'll be friends forever and ever, Willa. I'm sorry I ever kept any secrets from you. I'll share my face lotion with you for the rest of my days.*

But just as I'm about to ask Amara exactly *how* she found me—and how in the heck she was able to mount Macaroni all by herself with her twisted ankle (!), a gaggle of voices call out through the fat drops of rain.

"Willaaaaaa!"

Amara and I are suddenly surrounded by a herd of riders and horses. Through the moonlight, I see the bright smiles of Gwyneth, Everleigh, Noel, and Clementine. And is that . . .

"Pasquale?!"

His incandescent green eyes beam back at me through the light of the flashlight. Which I am now shining directly into his face.

"You're all here??"

"We came to rescue you!" Gwyneth trills from atop Romeo as Silver Streak whinnies a happy hello to the group.

"Look, Silver Streak is safe, and you're both soaking wet—just like in my vision!" Clementine exclaims from Aurora's saddle.

"Whoa—you really *do* have psychic powers," Amara says as we all stare, flabbergasted, at Clementine.

"My wrist tipped me off about the rain and the soaking-wet thing." She winks. "But I just *knew* you'd find Silver Streak. He's your heart-horse!"

"I can't believe you braved the Forsaken Forest twice in one day." I stroke Silver Streak's sopping mane to make sure he's staying calm amongst the hubbub.

"It was terrifying!" Noel confides, tightly gripping Tango's reins. "But we did it anyway."

"We'd never leave you stranded alone." Everleigh grins down from Sierra.

"That's what forever friends are for," Gwyneth adds.

I shoot a meaningful glance at Amara. She responds with one of her signature eye rolls. But I can see the corners of her lips lifting into a smile.

"But seriously, how did you find us?"

Pasquale leans over from his horse, Alfredo. He's shielding his eyes from the glaring beam of my flashlight, which is *still* shining in his face. I quickly lower it, just as he raises something to his lips and blows.

A soft, pathetic *heeeeeeeee* sound comes out—like a balloon deflating.

I tilt my head in confusion.

"We knew we had to get back to you and Amara quickly," Gwyneth explains. "So after we distracted Nora and the other counselors—"

"I told them we all had explosive food poisoning and that they should give us an hour of privacy in the bathroom!" Noel says proudly. "I was *so* convincing?"

"Then *I* told them we saw you and Amara walking down the road out of camp that leads to the highway," Everleigh continues. "Nora went running to find you—"

"In the exact opposite direction of the shack!" Noel finishes.

"Mr. Gulch was busy with these two mean-looking people who showed up at his office," Clementine adds.

"So then," Noel says breathlessly, "we decided to find Pasquale!"

"We knew he'd be able to navigate the secret trail better than anyone," Clementine explains. "Since he's been coming to Juniper Ranch—"

"Since *forever*," everyone singsongs in unison.

Pasquale raises an eyebrow. "Hey, it's true!"

"Pasquale offered to help us right away," Gwyneth says.

"Will brothers never cease," Amara deadpans.

"He showed us the way back down to the secret trail to where we left you at the creepy shack," Noel continues. "And that's when we found Amara!"

"She was holding her ankle and crying," Gwyneth says, glancing sympathetically at Amara.

"I was *not?*" Amara yelps. "It was just the drizzle."

"We brought Macaroni along with us since we knew Amara didn't have a horse to ride," Clementine explains.

"And then Pasquale and I lifted Amara up onto Macaroni's saddle so she wouldn't hurt her ankle!" Everleigh beams with pride.

"Hey, I work out." Pasquale makes a muscle with his arms. (I quickly look to the ground, as if his bicep is an eclipse I dare not glance at without protective eyewear.)

"So do I!" Everleigh adds, making an even larger muscle with her arm.

"Anyway," Gwyneth says, ignoring the dueling Popeye impressions. "We figured we'd be able to follow Silver Streak's heart prints to find you, Wills."

"But the rain had washed them away!" Clementine gasps.

"And that's when Pasquale showed us the horse whistle," Noel jumps in.

"You mean the most annoying sound on the planet?" Amara sneers. "Who brings a fake horse squeal whistle to camp anyway?"

"I don't know," Pasquale replies innocently. "Maybe a brother who wants to scare his stepsister during her first time at campfire ghorst stories??"

"I *knew* that was you." Amara points an accusing finger as he grins proudly.

"We thought that Bandit or Silver Streak—if you'd found him—would hear the whistle and whinny back . . . so we could follow the sound to find you," Gwyneth explains.

"Or, you know, whinny back and then run away into the creek in terror!" I say with a shaky laugh.

"The point is? We found you!" Noel claps her hands together in triumph.

"And Bandit!" Everleigh adds.

"And Silver Streak!" Amara coos, scratching the white star between his ears.

A low roll of thunder grumbles in the distance.

"Just so everybody knows," I clarify, "that was *not* my tummy."

CHAPTER FORTY-ONE

Eventually, the storm sails past us. Its ebbing clouds reveal a clear night sky that's studded with glittering stars. My eyes instinctively search for the Pegasus constellation to help guide us home.

When our bedraggled caravan finally arrives back at the Juniper Ranch barn, we're still soaked to the bone.

"We made it." Noel exhales with relief.

"*Shhhhh!*" Gwyneth shushes us. "Nobody's noticed we're back yet."

We silently dismount from our horses, knowing that the moment we're discovered, our adventure will be over. Finished. Done. *Finito. Completo.*

"No matter what happens, I'll never forget today," I whisper. "Or this summer. Or any of you."

"Same," Amara whispers back.

"Same," repeats a chorus of whispers.

"Group hug?" Pasquale asks cheekily.

(I thank the horse gods that it's nearly dark in this barn—except for a little moonlight filtering in from the rafters—so that nobody will notice my cheeks melting into molten lava.)

Still clinging to our horse reins, we gather in a circle and throw our arms around one another. A pang of heartsickness shoots through me as I realize this may be the last time we'll all be together. Our magical summer at horse camp is almost definitely over.

And I'm pretty sure *none* of us will ever be invited back again. 😔

After a long hug, our arms drop one by one. After all, barn chores never wait—even for horse girls (and boys) deep in their feelings.

We still have to get our damp steeds dry, cozy, and safe for the night. Which means picking their hooves, curry-combing their coats, putting their tack away, and filling all their bellies with hay (and NickerDoodles!) after this terrifying, wild, and wonderful day.

We work as a team to quickly groom each horse and get them settled for the night.

Then I personally check *three times* to make sure their stall doors are tightly latched. I'm not about to go searching through the forest for another horse who decides to nap himself tonight!

Eventually, the only steed left to tuck in is Silver Streak.

But just as Amara lures him back to his warm stall with the promise of a NickerDoodle, I hear the front barn doors fling open.

Pffffft! Silver Streak shifts his feet nervously as a woman's frantic voice echoes down the barn aisle.

"Well, it's nice of you to finally show up after all my phone calls. We should search the barn first!"

"Sure," a man's voice replies. "Wherever you'd like to start."

The overhead barn lights flick on, and we all hold our breaths.

"Mom??" Amara asks.

We all whip our heads around to find Amara's mother—and her giant handbag—standing in front of the barn doors, next to a man wearing thick glasses above a thick mustache.

"He must be here from the insurance company," Amara hisses, "to take Silver Streak."

"My baby!" Amara's mom gushes. She bounds over to embrace Amara, bonking the man with her giant purse in the process, then furiously smoothing Amara's eyebrows.

"You're here already?" Amara asks, her voice drenched with dread.

"Of course I am, sweetheart! After you sent me that *horrifying* photo of the ransom note, I came straight away. I was so worried about Silver Streak! And you, of course."

"We've *all* been worried," a gravelly voice hollers. I turn back to see Mr. Gulch striding through the open barn doors.

"I can explain everything, Mr. Gulch," I say, hoping to stem the giant tidal wave of trouble about to crash into us.

"Oh, you're all going to do *a lot* of explaining. You folks broke every single one of my rules this week. And then you broke some more!"

Noel zaps me a look, her eyes popping I-told-you-so wide.

"We'll discuss the consequences of your actions tomorrow." Mr. Gulch takes his hat off and exhales loudly, wiping his palms on his jeans. "But dagnabit, am I happy to see you all safe and sound."

Amara's mother, however, is focused entirely on Mr. Mustache.

"While it appears Silver Streak has been miraculously found—thank heavens—we still expect the insurance claim to be paid *fully*." She looks pointedly at the man with the glasses. "As I previously discussed with your supervisor, this horse will likely never be able to compete professionally again."

"Madam, I'm—"

But before he can finish, Nora bursts through the barn doors, her red curls bouncing behind her.

"You're here!" she says, choking back tears. "I was so bloody worried!"

My stomach tightens with guilt. I feel terrible that we sent Nora on a wild goose chase so she wouldn't realize we'd snuck into the Forsaken Forest. But Nora's distraught face quickly melts into a relieved smile.

"Blimey, am I happy to see you all . . . and this beautiful horsey!" She scratches Silver Streak's neck and begins scooping each of us (even Pasquale!) into a relieved hug.

"Speaking of the horsey—" Mr. Mustache says.

This time he's interrupted by Griff, who hustles in behind Nora and makes a beeline for Pasquale and his whistle.

"Hey, I was just *borrowing* it," Pasquale says as Griff tugs the whistle from Pasquale's neck and stuffs it into his pocket.

"Sure you were." Griff shakes his head. "We'll be having a conversation about maturity and pranks and large-animal noises later."

"We're well within our rights!" Amara's mom continues, ignoring every other conversation in the room.

"If I could just—" the man in the glasses tries again.

Boom!

The barn doors slam wide open again, startling us all.

"Will someone please explain *exactly* what's going on here??"

We fling our heads back to the stable's entrance to see who the voice belongs to this time.

Amara glances at Pasquale.

"Dad??"

Chapter Forty-Two

"Guilty!" the man says, as Amara dashes over to hug him, practically knocking him over.

He lets out a raucous laugh, and I notice his thick, dark hair is just as glossy as hers. He waves Pasquale over and throws an arm over him as well.

"Your mom texted me about some sort of horsenapping, so I drove here as fast I could."

"Because Silver Streak was napped!" Amara's mother pushes her giant purse in front of her like a shield as she marches over to join them.

Her father raises his eyebrows at Silver Streak, who's now looming over the family and nickering happily. "Sure seems to be *un*napped now."

"He is, Dad!" Amara says excitedly Then she nods at me. "Wills found him!"

He gives me a grateful smile. "Thank you for going above and beyond for my family, Willa Watkins."

(Whoa—Amara's dad knows my full name? Which means . . . she told him about me being her friend? Which means . . . she maybe, possibly, probably-not told Pasquale about me before horse camp??)

"And then all my other friends came to save us!" Amara sweeps her arm toward Gwyneth, Everleigh, Noel, and Clementine, who beam proudly.

Pasquale clears his throat. Loudly.

"Okay, okay." Amara grins. "And also Pasquale."

"I'm sure glad you two are getting along so well." Her dad smiles, then glances pointedly at Silver Streak. "In fact, it looks like *everybody's* safe and sound."

"We are *not* safe and sound." Amara's mom stamps her foot. "Silver Streak has gone lame! And this gentleman from the insurance company"—she stabs a bright red nail toward the man in the suit—"is refusing to take him back. Even though we had a *guarantee.*"

"That horse is fine." We all look over to Mr. Gulch, who shoves his hands in his jeans pockets.

"I beg to differ," Amara's mom whimpers. "Silver Streak has been diagnosed with *laminitis*. Our veterinarian put heart-bar shoes on him, for goodness' sake."

"Of course she did—those shoes are helping him heal," Mr. Gulch grumbles. "Plenty of horses with laminitis recover just dandy. I've been in this business enough decades to know that. You've just got to give the fella some time and patience. Oh sure, maybe he won't be jumping over high fences anytime soon—"

"Exactly!" Amara's mom pounces. "Did you hear that?"

She burns her deathly glare at Amara's father, and then the insurance man, going back and forth between the two.

"This . . . equine *expert,* who claims he's been in the business for *decades,* just testified that Silver Streak won't be able to jump over high fences anytime soon."

"I really don't—"

The man tries to jump in, but Amara's mom blocks him with a key change, raising her voice a few notes higher.

"Which *proves* that he's no longer worth the value we paid! Which is why we bought the insurance policy in the first place!"

Her fingernail stabs higher in the air, matching the octave of her voice.

"We bought the insurance to help cover any *emergencies,*" Amara's dad says evenly.

"This *is* an emergency. Amara needs to be jumping high fences immediately if we want to keep on track for the US Equestrian team and"—Amara's mom lets out a thrilled gasp—"eventually the Olympics!"

But her face softens as she looks over at Amara.

"Sweetheart, I know you love Silver Streak. We all do. We

just want you to have a horse who's healthy—and safe—to jump."

Amara buries her face in Silver Streak's glorious side bangs. It looks like her heart might crack right open in front of all of us.

"Your father and I both just want the best for you," Amara's mom adds gently.

Her father shakes his head. "Maybe we should ask Amara what *she* wants."

Amara looks up at him, then at Silver Streak, then at every other face in the barn. Her eyes lock with mine for a moment. I give her an encouraging nod and point to my bracelet.

After a moment, she takes a breath and nods back.

"Silver Streak is part of my forever herd," Amara says firmly. "I honestly don't care if we can jump or even trot again. I just never, ever want to lose him. So I'll find a way to protect him, even if it's really hard. Even if it means we can't compete together. Even if it means *I* don't compete again."

Amara's mother lets out a horrified gasp that rattles through the stable rafters.

"If I could just interrupt—" The man with the glasses clears his throat and tries again.

"I'll never let you take him!" Amara yelps, leaping in front of Silver Streak and throwing her arms out protectively.

"Whoa, whoa, whoa," Mr. Mustache says, stumbling

backward and raising his hands in surrender. "I'm not here to take your horse, I promise."

Amara narrows her eyes at him. "You're not?"

"No." He chuckles, raising his thick eyebrows over his glasses as he glances back at Nora and Mr. Gulch. "I'm here to film a movie!"

CHAPTER FORTY-THREE

"Everybody, meet Francis Cooperman!" Nora booms, gesturing to the man with the thick mustache and glasses. "Mr. Cooperman directed the last two films Balthazar and I worked on. He was looking for a location for his next movie, so I suggested Juniper Ranch!"

Blimey.

"It's absolutely perfect, just *perfect*," the director enthuses, pumping Mr. Gulch's hand and gazing admiringly around the barn.

"Golly, am I happy to hear that," Mr. Gulch says, relief filling his voice. "That location fee is going to keep our little camp afloat for quite a while."

"Excellent, excellent!" Mr. Cooperman says, holding his hands in front of his eyes like it's a camera lens. "I can see this thing becoming a trilogy."

He glances back at Nora. "We'll also need a few more

stunt riders and horses if you know of anyone who might be interested?"

Nora looks over at us and winks, and we all nod enthusiastically back to her. "I expect I might have a few ideas."

But Amara's mother swoops in first. She smooths her eyebrows, adjusts the giant handbag on her arm, and stretches a hand toward the director.

"I'm actually a former professional rider, Mr. Cooperman," she swans. "And a *huge* fan of your work. I'd just love to lend a hand with your picture?"

"Fantastic, fantastic," he says, still staring through the fake camera frame of his fingers. "I'll have my people set up an audition with your people when I'm back at the end of the summer."

Amara's mom puffs up her shoulders, clearly pleased with herself, as Amara turns to me with a gigantic loop-di-loop of an eye roll.

"Just one condition," Mr. Cooperman says after a pause, finally glancing up. "You've got to keep that horse. He's the perfect star for my movie!"

CHAPTER FORTY-FOUR

The rest of the summer flies by in the blink of an eye. It's a blur of trail rides, creek swims, sunset singalongs, gallons of "bug juice," tons of friendship bracelets, and way too many tummy flip-flops to count (especially when Pasquale wears the TAIL-OR SWIFT shirt I made him). Not to mention . . . HORSES, HORSES, HORSES!

Mr. Gulch said we could *try* to earn back his trust by doing a gazillion barn chores and volunteering with the younger campers in Pony Pals and Rainbow Dash. The funny thing is? This "punishment" is one of my all-time favorite parts of camp! I *adore* teaching the junior riders all the skills I've learned in the last year at Juniper Ranch and Oakwood.

When one of the youngest Pony Pals campers gets homesick, I show her my GRIT bracelet, explaining what it means. Then I get Bandit to stick his tongue out at Mr. Gulch when he walks past, and we laugh so hard that I almost have a bathroom emergency.

It feels good to help someone else navigate the seriously *unfun* things I've already dealt with in my life. (Whoa. Is this how my big sister Kay feels all the time??)

Oh, and when the real horse insurance agent eventually shows up? We tell him there's been a terrible mix-up. (Then Mr. Cooperman tries to cast him as the villain in his next movie, ha!) Fortunately, Amara's mom agrees to let Silver Streak stay at Juniper Ranch for the rest of the summer, resting and relaxing until he's 100 percent healed and cleared by the vet before Mr. Cooperman starts filming.

"I'll pay for anything he needs!" Amara's mom says fervently. "He's got to be ready for his close-up. Our Silver Streak could be the next It horse!"

CHAPTER FORTY-FIVE

Pffffffft.

Bandit gives me a quick nuzzle as I slip into his stall. I waited until everyone else was finished tacking up their steeds this morning so that Bandit's Camp Games costume would be a surprise.

"Good morning, buddy!" I say brightly, brushing his blond bangs out of his eyes. "Are you ready for our big last day together?"

Bandit nickers and begins to bob his head in what looks like a yes, then shakes his mane in what seems to be a no.

Maybe all of his happys keep getting mixed up with his sads, too . . . just like mine. Or maybe he was just trying to shake off a fly. Either way, we're both dealing with some big feelings this morning.

"Since you and I both come from military families, I guess we've both had to get used to goodbyes." I drape a pad and saddle over his back and tighten the girth, willing myself to focus on the task in front of me—instead of the salty sting of tears I feel forming in my throat.

"I'm going to miss you so much, boy," I whisper, as a few teardrops cascade down my cheeks. "You made this my best summer *ever*, despite all the scary things we had to face. Like thunderstorms. And lost friends."

Bandit stamps his foot.

"And yes—I almost forgot—terrifying pine cones!" I giggle, stroking his forelock. "I'm so lucky you were my halter-ego."

Bandit *pfffffffffts* again, and I throw my arms around his neck.

"I promise I'll come back so we can do it all again next summer," I say, before heaving a sigh. "That is if Mr. Gulch doesn't ban me from horse camp for life."

Which reminds me of my other Big Worry.

My dad will be here soon to pick me up. And tell me the "big news" he mentioned in his letter. Which I've tried to forget about all summer. And which absolutely, positively *cannot* be good.

I look into Bandit's eyes and then down at my bracelet. I only have a few precious hours left with my fellow campers and my beloved summer steed. I better make 'em count.

"Let's get you dressed," I say, forcing a smile as I give Bandit's muzzle a quick kiss. "We've got some Camp Games to win!"

When Bandit and I reach the outdoor riding ring, the other Juniper Ranch campers and their steeds are waiting for us. Bandit snorts and whinnies with happiness—he can feel the energy in the air.

I've woven a pink feather boa down his mane, draped another one from his tail, and completely covered his coat with pink Pony Paint.

Voilà—I am now riding a pink flamingo!

"Good on ya, gang!" Nora claps her hands approvingly at our giddy-up getups.

I turn Bandit in a circle so I can admire my campmates and their wild kingdom of steeds.

Gwyneth, Everleigh, and Noel have used Pony Paint to transform their matching paints—Romeo, Sierra, and Tango—into triplet giraffes. Clementine has crafted a golden horn out of a paper-towel roll and sparkly glitter to turn Aurora into a magical unicorn—complete with a flowing, purple Pony Paint mane to match her own hair.

The junior Juniper Ranch campers, meanwhile, are trotting around on a menagerie of mountain lions. (Too soon!)

As for the boys of King of the Wind? They've disguised their horses as a herd of Santa's reindeer, using fake antler headbands made with sticks from the campfire and jingle bells from the Craft Shack. Pasquale's horse, Alfredo, even has a red nose, just like Rudolph!

He catches me staring at him, and I instantly blush the color of Rudolph's beak.

"I better see you at camp next year, Mane Character Energy." Pasquale winks at me as he says this. (At least I think he was winking at me? It's possible he just has unicorn glitter in his eye.)

OMG. OMG.

Did Pasquale just invite me back to camp next summer?? *ARE WE GETTING SERIOUS?!?*

He trots back to his friends before I can ask. Guess I'll find out in twelve months!

That is, if my parents haven't forced me to move to the other side of the planet by then. *Ugh.* And if I can somehow find a way to pay for camp next year. *Double ugh.* Which reminds me . . . I need to thank Amara one last time for dreaming up a scholarship that completely changed my life.

But when I glance around at the ring full of riders, I don't see her magnificent glossy hair anywhere. Or Silver Streak's magnificent side bangs.

Oh no. Did Amara's mom change her mind about turning Silver Streak into a Hollywood A-lister??

After a few moments, the reindeer herd parts . . . and my eyes find Amara, charging through the sea of antlers. Huh, why does she look so much shorter than normal?

I quickly realize that instead of Silver Streak, Amara is

riding (*looooooow*) atop Macaroni the pony! Who she's dressed up as a tiny pink mouse, complete with pink felt ears and pink mouse pants, stitched from her Barbie-pink comforter.

"He may be small, but he is mighty!" she says proudly. "I decided to ride him for Camp Games so Silver Streak can keep resting before filming begins. Turns out Macaroni's got spunk!"

Right on cue, Amara urges Macaroni into a trot, then a canter, zipping in a tiny pink blur past all of us.

"Move it or lose it, breeches!" she laughs giddily.

"That's my baby!" a woman's voice calls out. "Excellent form, Amara!"

I look over to see Amara's smiling mom, standing just beside the riding ring. She's holding Silver Streak's lead rope and gently brushing his choppy mane into place.

Mr. Cooperman stands next to them, framing all the costumed horses between his hands. "Yes, yes, we'll film the grand finale right here!"

"Will there be any jumping in your movie?" Amara's mom trills. "Because as you may know, I was a member of the 1999 US Equestrian Junior Jumping Team."

"In that case, I may just have to add some scenes to the script," Mr. Cooperman murmurs.

Amara's mom looks like she might levitate off the ground with happiness.

"And perhaps a grandmotherly-type rider!" Mr. Cooperman exclaims.

She opens her mouth to protest, but Nora's booming voice interrupts her.

"Attention, Juniper campers! Time to line up with your cabinmates!"

Bandit and I gather with the Misty riders and their horses as we watch Amara finish her speedy whirl around the outdoor ring.

"I'm so glad Silver Streak will get to come back to Oakwood after Mr. Cooperman's movie." Gwyneth grins.

"I just wish you could come back with us, too, Clem," Everleigh laments. "Since you're now an *official* Oakwood Flyer."

"Me too," Noel sighs.

"Our spirits will meet again soon on another astral plane," Clementine says serenely, closing her eyes.

"Another psychic vision?" Everleigh asks.

Clementine nods before flicking her eyes open. "Because my dad said I could come visit from California!"

We whoop and giggle as Amara and Macaroni the Mouse trot over to us.

"What's so funny??" she asks in a panic. "Was my seat off?"

"Your seat was as annoyingly perfect as always, Amara!" I reassure her.

CHAPTER FORTY-SIX

"Greetings, parents, campers, and friends! Welcome to Juniper Ranch's annual Camp Games!" Mr. Gulch's voice echoes gruffly through a portable microphone. "As you can see, we've got the entire animal kingdom gathered today!"

Dozens of parents chuckle from the stack of metal bleachers Mr. Gulch has set up on the side of the field. They point out the ramshackle costumes we campers have stitched, spackled, and bedazzled together.

The arena buzzes with energy as we sit excitedly atop our horses, huddled together at one end of the arena.

"These young riders have worked diligently during their time at camp to become responsible horsewomen and horsemen. Today, they're going to show you some of the skills they've learned, the teamwork they've built, and a little bit of the fun they've been having at Juniper Ranch. And with that . . . may the games begin!"

Cheers and whoops ring out from the stands.

"Looking good, Amara!" her father's voice calls out.

"Way to go, girls!" the Claremont triplets' mother shouts. "Triple threat!"

"Your aura is so energized!" cries another parent, who most certainly must belong to Clementine.

My eyes dart around the crowd, searching for my dad and Kay.

Nora grabs the mic and announces that we'll start with a mounted game of Red Light, Green Light. We're instructed to trot ahead on our horses when she turns her back—and then screech to a halt whenever she flips around to face us.

"Alfredo and I are gonna win this whole thing!" Pasquale boasts.

"Not if Macaroni and I have anything to say about it!" Amara shouts back playfully.

I scan the bleachers, grinning excitedly as I imagine my dad and Kay watching an entire herd of horses in costumes playing lawn games while a famous movie director watches in the background. I bet my dad is already practicing his best "There's no business like horse business!" joke as we speak.

"Green light!" Nora calls, and we all dash ahead.

"Red light!" she shouts, twirling around and tagging out any horse and rider who are still moving.

I try to peek through the clump of riders and horses surrounding me, but I see no sign of Kay's frizzy hair and glasses. Or my dad's HORSE DAD ON DUTY visor and clip-on sunglasses.

Then it hits me. And my heart (literally) sinks in my chest.

My dad is *never* late. Which means something's seriously wrong. Which means . . . my parents' "big news"? Must have already begun.

Ughhhhhhh.

I'm suddenly certain that my mom's deployment has already been extended—and that my dad is already packing us up for our next move. Kay will be going to college soon, so I'll be *completely* alone in another new town.

"Green light!" Nora screams.

The other horses and riders amble forward, but I keep Bandit frozen in place. I feel dizzy and lost—there's no way I can keep going. Not when my life as a horse girl is about to be officially over. For real this time.

"Green means go, Willa!" a familiar voice shouts.

As the other hooves gallop past me, I steal one more glance back at the stands. And that's when I see them.

Three figures walking hand in hand through the gates.

My dad, Kay, and . . .

MOM!!!!!!!!!

CHAPTER FORTY-SEVEN

"MOM!!!!!" I cry again, as soon as the Camp Games have finished and Bandit and I can run into her arms. "You're here!"

I'm wearing a blue ribbon from the mounted egg race. As well as a big yellow stain on my shirt from said egg race.

"Oh, Willa, it is so wonderful to get to squeeze you, scrambled eggs and all!" She grins so widely that the freckles dance on her cheeks. "I am *so* proud of you and this incredible summer of yours."

"Well, hello to you too, kiddo!" my dad laughs, wrapping his arm around me.

"Sorry—hi, Dad! Hi, Kay!" I remember to say, wiping tears of happiness from my eyes.

I give them a giant hug, then point to the beautiful steed standing next to me. "Family, meet Bandit!"

Bandit neighs loudly, right on cue.

"He reminds me of Dolly Parton, Mom!" I explain excitedly.

"He definitely looks like one tough blond," she says in her booming, sunny voice.

"Yeah, he's actually pretty cute," Kay deadpans. "For livestock." She reaches up to brush his forelock—then promptly sneezes.

"Good old Clyde Lee might be jealous when you get home and he hears you made a new buddy at camp," my dad chuckles.

"When we get *home*?" I ask, my tone turning gloomy. "Is this the part where you tell me we're moving again because Mom has another deployment? And that I'm never going to get to go back to Oakwood *or* Juniper Ranch?"

"Whoa, whoa, whoa, Sebastian." My dad puts his hands in the air.

I glare at him in confusion.

"Wanna know why I'm calling you Sebastian?"

I give him an annoyed shrug.

"Because you're acting pretty crabby." He grins, clearly proud of his *Little Mermaid* joke. "Maybe that shoulda been your costume today!"

My mom puts her arm on my shoulder. "Willa, why on earth would you think we're moving again?"

"Because you said in the letter you had *big news*!" I say desperately. "Which always means the same thing in this family. I'm going to have to give up all my people friends and my horse friends and start over somewhere new and—"

"Now wait just one gosh-darn minute," my dad interrupts. "Did we get a single letter from you this entire summer, Wills?"

"Ummm," I stammer.

"I sent several." Kay smiles smugly.

"Sorry! I kind of had a lot going on this summer!" (If only they knew . . .)

"Well, if we *had* gotten a letter back and you'd told us your big worries about our big news," my mom says in her *I'm serious young lady* voice, "then we may have been able to share it with you sooner."

"Share what with me sooner?"

My mom's face explodes into a giant smile. "I'm retiring!" she squeals. "No more moves. Nebraska is going to be our forever home."

"We'll all be together again, Willa," my dad says, as he tries to wipe away the tears filling his eyes. "My three girls under one roof."

"Well, at least until I go to college," Kay sniffs. But then she throws her arm around us—even wrapping Bandit into our family hug, and sealing it with a sneeze.

As we hold each other tight and I see my campmates smiling at us in the distance, my heart longs to stay frozen in this moment. Why can't everyone I love just stay in one place . . . forever?

I glance down at my bracelet, and then I remember.

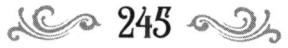

Even though your friends sometimes change (or go missing!), and your mom sometimes has to work on the other side of the planet, and your sister eventually has to leave for college, and your dad forces you to pack a flashlight because he can't always be there to light the way for you himself, and your favorite steed can't always ride with you, and you sometimes have to do *really* hard things all by yourself . . . you can still bring those people and places and horses and bracelets with you. Inside your heart.

While you keep riding bravely ahead.

Thud.

My deep thoughts are interrupted by the sound of boots thudding in the dirt. I look up to see a cowboy hat bobbing closer to us.

"Excuse me, folks," Mr. Gulch says. "Hate to interrupt the family reunion, but I have something very important to discuss with you."

Oh no. Mr. Gulch is about to tell my parents what happened—and kick me out of horse camp. On the very last day of horse camp! How mortifying is that??

"Your daughter . . ."

Gulp.

"Is one of the bravest riders I've ever met," he continues. "She has a real gift with the junior campers."

Wait, what?

"I was wondering if she might want to come back next summer?"

"That's incredibly kind of you, Mr. Gulch," my mom says.

"We'll just have to check the old budget." My dad lets out a whistle. "You've got a pretty fancy place here, Mr. Gulch!"

"Oh, I was hoping she'd come back as a counselor-in-training, with the rest of her pals." Mr. Gulch grins. "Since Nora and Griff have decided to work together as team stunt riders on Mr. Cooperman's movie, I'm going to need some new staff. We'll of course pay them. I have a feeling these horse girls have a lot to teach the younger riders about wilderness riding survival skills."

He gives me a wink as my parents shake his hand.

OMG.

OMG.

OMGeeeeeeeee.

I'M GOING TO HORSE CAMP!!!!

Acknowledgments

This book exists only because of the endless generosity of my favorite horse camp bunkmate, Lindsay Seim. My sister and I shared two magical summers as Silver Spurs riders and the rest of our childhood inventing our own *Clue*-inspired mysteries. This story is as much hers as mine. Thank you, Lindsay, for riding lead in my forever herd.

Thanks to my beloved champion Brian Clark for insisting I say yes, for sharing your genius, for bringing me along on all the best adventures. To my ride-or-die, Clarké Adams. What would I do without your steady wit and careful eye? Everything is better since you jumped into my life.

I'm indebted to author-whisperer Elizabeth Lee for your savvy and gentle guidance, and to the brilliant Penguin Workshop team—fearlessly led by Francesco Sedita and Rob Valois—for giving me a go at yet another rodeo.

To my agents, Merrilee Heifetz and Mary Pender, I'm

honored and thrilled to have you at the reins. The unbridled enthusiasm of our #HorseGirl team—including the magical Zosia Mamet, Heather Wordham, Sally Ware, Rebecca Eskildsen, and Celia Albers—leaves me in awe.

Many thanks to two gifted veterinarians, Dr. Sarah Adams and Dr. Lueen Mansfield, for sharing your expertise and horse love. Thank you to the entire whip-smart Adams family—especially Paige, Colin, and Tristan—for graciously welcoming me into your herd. And for introducing me to the breathtaking beauty (and shenanigans!) of trail rides in the mountains.

To Steph Waldo for your work-of-art covers that leap off the page, Ron Baird for the snazzy camp map, and Mary Claire Cruz, our design wizard. Thank you to OG #HorseBoy Karl Jones for your giant leap of faith. To Kate Gardiner of Grey Horse for pulling off several miracles. To Number One wrangler David Watkins and the Willett, Parsons, and Cray families for always lighting the way.

I'm grateful to several lifesaving squads, especially teachers and librarians, Thor and Athena's Promise (an incredible Colorado horse sanctuary—please support if you can!), Gallop NYC, and the spectacular BreyerFest team, led by Jaime Potkalesky and Kathryn McDermott.

To my stable of writer and editor pals who champion and challenge me: horse-author extraordinaire Sarah Maslin Nir, Aussie fact-checkers Emma Sloley and Adam McCulloch, Trent Preszler (who built the canoe that started it all!), Katie

Rosman, Matthew Aldrich, Jane Smiley, Soledad O'Brien, Elizabeth Letts, Pat Miller, Patrick Vaill, Mackenzie Dawson, DeMarco Williams, Hailey Eber, Christina Amoroso, April Daniels Hussar, Holly Caccamise, Shweta Jha, Heather Alexander, Kat Lambrix, Thomas Mann, Brandon T. Snider, Sherine Tadros, Ayman Mohyeldin, Wendi McLendon-Covey, Tom Lenk, Tracy Bitterolf, Joe Miale, and Reed Levine.

Above all, thank you to my parents, Don and Sharon Seim, who let me go to horse camp even though I was really, *really* allergic. Who read to me every night of my childhood. Who've read (and reread) every word I've written with unwavering delight. *How deep is the ocean, how high is the sky?*